Hannah and the Special 4th of July

Best Friends

#4

Hannah and the Special 4th of July

Hilda Stahl

CROSSWAY BOOKS • WHEATON, ILLINOIS
A DIVISION OF GOOD NEWS PUBLISHERS

*Jonathan, this is for you
with love always*

Hannah and the Special 4th of July.

Copyright © 1992 by Word Spinners, Inc.

Published by Crossway Books, a division of
Good News Publishers, 1300 Crescent Street, Wheaton, Illinois 60187.

Cover illustration: Paul Casale

First printing, 1992

Printed in the United States of America

Library of Congress Cataloging-in-Publication Data
Stahl, Hilda.
    Hannah and the special 4th of July / Hilda Stahl.
       p.   cm. — (Best friends : #4)
    Summary: Hannah struggles with her Native American heritage
especially after her cousin comes to visit and questions her involvement
with the King's Kids and her acceptance of Jesus as her Savior.
    [1. Indians of North America—Fiction. 2. Cousins—Fiction.
3. Christian life—Fiction.] I. Title. II. Title: Hannah and the
special fourth of July. III. Series: Stahl, Hilda. Best friends : #4.
PZ7.S78244Han 1992   [Fic]—dc20   91-43089
ISBN 0-89107-660-3

00	99	98	97	96	95	94	93
15	14	13	12	11	10	9	8	7	6	5	4	3

Contents

1

The Terrible Surprise

Smiling, Hannah pulled the money pouch from her dresser drawer. She was going to meet her best friends—Chelsea, Roxie, and Kathy—in a few minutes, but first she had to count the *King's Kids* finances. She was the treasurer. It was wonderful having best friends, and it was fun to be treasurer. She glanced up and caught her reflection in the mirror, and her smile disappeared. Her face was broad and dark, her black hair straight and coarse, and her eyes as black as coal. She was Ottawa. "I could never pass as a white girl," she whispered in anguish. Then she frowned. She was proud to be Ottawa!

Slowly she walked to the small square table in the corner of the bedroom she shared with Lena. Hannah sank down on the chair. The summer would last only two more months, and then school would start again. How long would it take Chelsea,

Roxie, and Kathy to realize they'd made a major mistake in having *her* as a best friend? Some people were beginning to admire Native Americans, but many still looked down on them—looked down on *her*. It had been very hard for their family to buy a house at The Ravines, and it had been harder still for her to make friends in that subdivision. Just before school was out for the summer, Chelsea had moved in across the street. The McCreas had come from Oklahoma, and Chelsea had always been around Native Americans. Hannah smiled as she thought of red-haired, freckled Chelsea McCrea. She wasn't prejudiced at all! Because of her Hannah had been accepted by Roxie Shoulders and Kathy Aber. The four of them were now best friends. And they all four were in the *King's Kids* business venture, along with six other kids. They did odd jobs around the neighborhood. Their motto was, "Great or small, we do it all."

Hannah spread the money out on the small table. If it hadn't been for Chelsea, she wouldn't have been allowed into the group. And she'd have never been voted in as treasurer even though she was good in math and made change correctly and easily.

Sighing heavily, Hannah put quarters in one pile, dimes in another, and nickles in another. All her life she'd yearned for a best friend. Now she had three. But for how long? She groaned. Could she go back to being a lonely Ottawa girl left out of everything? Tears stung the backs of her eyes as she shook her head. It would be terrible to suffer the loneliness she'd felt before Chelsea McCrea moved in across the street.

Just then Lena ran into the room. She stopped short and stared at the money. Her black eyes gleamed. "Is that for Daddy's birthday present?"

Hannah shook her head as she struggled to be patient. "I wish it was." His birthday was July 16, and she'd only saved four dollars for his gift. "Why are you in here? I thought you were going to play with the twins." They were eight and often left nine-year-old Lena out of their play.

Lena crossed her arms and looked ready to cry. "They always have secrets they want to share with each other. Why won't they ever share their secrets with me?"

"That's just the way they are." Hannah stacked the money in piles of a dollar each. She'd thought she'd have the room to herself for a while. How she wished she had a room of her own! In a few days it would be even worse. Mom had said that just after the 4th of July family gathering the twins would move in with her and Lena, so they could use the twins' room as a nursery for Burke, her baby brother. The bedroom was plenty big enough for four girls, and it was decorated beautifully with matching multicolored spreads and curtains. Shelves lined one side of the wall and were full of colorful stuffed animals and games and toys. The carpet was the same blue as in the spreads and curtains. But still, she wouldn't have any privacy then.

Lena sighed as she leaned against the table. "Don't you ever wish we didn't have Vivian and Sherry?"

Hannah had often wished they didn't have the twins—or Lena for that matter—but she didn't say so. "We have them, and that's all there is to it."

Lena tugged at the neckline of her yellow T-shirt. "Did you ever wish you were a twin so you would have someone your age to talk to?"

"Yes."

"Now you have three best friends," said Lena, sounding envious. "I don't have a best friend. Hannah, do you think I'll ever have a best friend?"

Hannah didn't know how to answer that without making Lena feel worse than she already did. It would take a miracle for Lena to find a best friend. But then a miracle had happened when Chelsea had moved in. Another one could happen for Lena. "Ask Jesus for a best friend, Lena."

"I have! I pray every single day for a best friend! How long will it take for an answer?"

"I don't know. But don't give up."

Lena tightened the wide red band that held her long hair in a ponytail down her thin back. "I'll hate having the twins in here all the time. Why can't Burke sleep in here with us?"

"He'd keep us up at night."

"It's not fair that he'll get a room all to himself." Lena sighed. "Hannah, I wish I had a room to myself. I'm nine years old and I've never had a room of my own."

"I know." Hannah tried again to count the money. Each of the *King's Kids* gave 2 percent of their earnings to help cover the cost of advertising and other expenses. Right now Lena's interruptions were making her job impossible. "Leave me alone, Lena. I have work to do."

Lena walked to her bed and flung herself down on it. Her blue shorts matched the blue in the bedspread. "Nobody ever wants to play with me! Everybody hates me!"

Hannah forced herself to ignore Lena. Finally Hannah finished counting the money, wrote the amount in her book, and scooped the money back into the pouch. "See you later, Lena." Hannah put the pouch in her dresser, touched her *I'm A Best Friend* button which was pinned to her T-shirt to make sure it was there, and walked into the hall. The phone rang, and she jumped. She answered it before it woke up Burke or Mom.

"Hi, Hannah, it's Ginny."

Hannah sank weakly against the wall. Why would her cousin call? They had never gotten along even though they were the same age. They saw each other only twice a year at family gatherings or pow-

11

wows. Ginny was mean and obnoxious. "Hi, Ginny. Did you want to talk to my mom or my dad?"

"No . . . You."

Hannah stifled a moan. "I'm listening."

"I am going to stay a few days with you after the family gathering. I talked to Uncle Burke, and he said I could."

"When did you talk to my dad?"

"Just a while ago . . . At work . . . He said to call and let you know so you could get the house ready."

Hannah thought of the lack of privacy now—and how much worse it would be with Ginny there. Why was Ginny going to stay a while? Was she causing problems again for her family? "I'll have the house ready," Hannah said stiffly.

"I hear a cute boy moved in across the street."

"He's twelve."

"So am I."

"He's a white boy."

"Good. I like white boys. See you in a few days."

"Bye." Hannah slammed down the receiver.

"What's wrong?" asked Lena from the bedroom doorway.

Hannah rolled her eyes. "Cousin Ginny will be staying with us for a few days!"

Lena groaned. "Why?"

"She didn't say."

"She's in some kind of trouble, I bet." Lena hiked up her shorts and rested her hands on her skinny hips. "Why can't she go somewhere else when she gets in trouble?"

"I guess nobody else will take her."

"Dad's got a soft heart."

"Too soft," muttered Hannah as she hurried downstairs. She was going to be late for the *King's Kids* meeting.

Outdoors the July sun burned down on her as she dashed across the quiet street to Chelsea's house. All the houses at The Ravines were built the same— two-story with a deck out back, a double-car garage, and nice-sized lawns with trees. Their house was the only one that had a giant rock near the sidewalk. The builders had uncovered it when they'd dug the basement. Mom had wanted to keep the rock as a decoration for the yard.

Hannah found the girls sitting in the backyard in the shade of the maples. They all wore shorts and T-shirts with *I'm A Best Friend* buttons pinned over their hearts. They smiled and said hi. Chelsea, president of *King's Kids*, was short and slight, blue-eyed, redheaded, and covered with freckles. Roxie, the secretary, was tall and thin. She had dark hair, cut short, and brown eyes. The vice president, Kathy, was medium height and weight with naturally curly blonde hair and blue eyes that sometimes looked hazel.

Hannah dropped cross-legged to the grass between Roxie and Kathy. They formed a circle, their bare knees almost touching. Gracie, a small brown dog that liked to tear up flower beds, ran into the yard, barked, then raced away. "Sorry I'm late," Hannah said breathlessly.

"No problem," Chelsea told her.

"Did you have to take care of your baby brother?" asked Kathy.

"No. Lena kept pestering me. Then I got this really rotten call from my cousin Ginny. She's going to stay with us a few days!"

"What's so rotten about her?" asked Roxie eagerly. Roxie sometimes liked to see what was wrong in someone else. It was sort of a hobby.

"She's spoiled and always in trouble." Hannah picked up a leaf and studied it as if it were the most important thing in the world. Finally she looked up. "She hates being Native American. She'd do anything to pass as white, but she looks Ottawa just like I do."

"Maybe we can help her while she's here," Chelsea said.

Hannah nodded, not really believing it was possible. The Best Friends had formed a pact to do good deeds, so she wouldn't tell them not to try. She wanted to change the subject. She turned to Roxie. "Did you do any more work on your carving?"

Roxie sighed. "I got the squirrel's tail done. Sometimes I don't think I can do it."

"You can!" Hannah cried. She'd love to have such talent.

"I worked on it about an hour today, but I really don't want to talk about it."

"I want to talk about Brody Vangaar," Kathy said. "He practically lives with us! I get really really tired of having him around all the time."

"Your dad wants to help him just like my dad wants to help Ginny. At least you like Brody." Hannah bit her lip. Would they think she was terrible for not liking her own cousin?

"He's all right, I guess." Kathy pulled her knees up to her chest. "It's just that he's always there!"

"Have any of you seen the jeans on sale at Jadal's?" Chelsea retied her sneaker, then looked up with a sheepish grin. "Sorry, Kathy. I couldn't help thinking about the jeans. I want them so badly! Oh, if only I could pay my phone bill and have enough money for the jeans too!"

"What about the money Betina Quinn paid us?" Hannah asked.

"I had to put all of it on my bill," Chelsea said, sighing. "It was hard to do. But Dad says I have to pay the bill first. I know he's right. I guess he's right." Chelsea wrinkled her nose. "I sure don't think he's right, but I still have to do it." She'd started *King's Kids* just to pay the phone bill she'd made calling her best friend in Oklahoma. The others had felt it was such a good idea they'd asked to join too.

"Want to have the meeting now?" Hannah questioned as she pulled a paper from the pocket of her tan shorts.

Chelsea nodded. "The *King's Kids* meeting will now come to order. Roxie, read the minutes from the last meeting."

Roxie flipped open her notebook and read, "In the last meeting we voted to take pay for cleaning Betina Quinn's house instead of having it be a good deed like Kathy wanted. She decided taking pay was fine to do. We also voted to use some of our money in the treasury to buy a card and a gift for Ezra Menski for his birthday July 4th. He doesn't have a family here in Middle Lake. We are nice to him even if he does let Gracie, his dog, ruin flowers."

"How much money is in the treasury?" Chelsea asked.

Hannah smoothed out the paper. "Fifteen dollars."

"How much can we spend on a gift?" Kathy inquired.

"Ten," Hannah said. "The rest must go to pay for the last flyers we had printed."

"Any suggestions on what to buy?" Chelsea looked at the others with her red brows raised almost to her bangs.

"A muzzle for Gracie," Roxie answered with a giggle.

"Seriously," Chelsea said, but she giggled too.

"How about a carving done by Roxie?" Hannah smiled at Roxie. "He likes to carve, and he already has something your grandpa made."

Roxie flushed. "I would never let him see my work! He'd think it was done by an amateur."

Chelsea jabbed Roxie's leg. "He knows you're not a professional yet."

"Suggest something else," Roxie snapped. "No way am I going to carve anything for Ezra Menski to see!"

"Maybe we could take dinner to him with a birthday cake and everything," Hannah suggested. "My granddad always liked that." "Granddad" was her great-grandpa, and he'd died several months earlier.

"Good idea!" Roxie nodded.

"We'll bake the cake ourselves," Chelsea said excitedly. "And we'll see if your mom will decorate it, Roxie. She does fantastic work!"

"I think she'd do it."

"It's settled." Chelsea tapped Roxie's notebook. "Write it down. We'll meet together in the morning of the third at my house and bake the cake. When it's cool we'll take it to Roxie's house to have it decorated." Chelsea turned to Hannah. "You buy the card and whatever we need for the cake." She looked from one girl to the other. "Any more business?"

"No," they said together, then giggled.

"The meeting is closed, and now we can talk Best Friends Club business. What's the special Bible verse for today, Hannah?"

Hannah clapped her hand to her mouth.

"Did you forget?" asked Roxie sharply.

Hannah nodded. She had never forgotten *King's Kids* or Best Friends business before. How could she now when she wanted to do everything just right so they wouldn't drop her once school started? "I'm sorry," she whispered, feeling close to tears.

"That's all right." Kathy patted Hannah's knee. "I have one. It's a part of Psalm 100, verse 3: 'The Lord made us and we are His.'"

The words wrapped around Hannah's heart and warmed her to the very core of her being. She was Ottawa, but the Lord made her and she belonged to Him! She smiled at her best friends, and they smiled back.

But then she thought about Ginny, and her heart sank.

2

Hannah's Special Dress

At Mom's call Hannah ran to the living room. She'd been home only a few minutes after helping the Best Friends at the Crandall house—a job they were doing together for the entire summer. Mom was sitting alone in the living room with her head back and her eyes closed. The twins and Lena were playing in the front yard. Baby Burke was asleep. "You called, Mom?"

"It came!" Mom pushed herself up from the rocking chair.

Hannah's eyes sparkled. "It did?"

"It's on the couch." Mom tugged her blouse down over her shorts. "I wanted to open it, but I stopped myself. I knew you'd want to."

Hannah reached for the box Great-grandma had promised to send in time for the 4th of July gathering. It was a very special dress Great-grandma had worn when she was twelve. Hannah had been working on a dress she'd made herself, but when Great- grandma called, she decided to put away that dress and wait for this one.

Her heart in her mouth, Hannah tore open the box and lifted out another box. She opened it, her hands trembling. Finally she saw the dress. It was made of fine tanned leather and was covered with beautiful beadwork. It had fringe at the sleeves and around the hem. She held it against herself as she looked at Mom for her reaction.

"What workmanship!" Mom whispered, gently touching the beadwork around the neckline.

"It's beautiful!" Hannah lifted the four-inch fringe and let it fall through her fingers.

"Since it's not a ceremonial dress, Great-grandma says you can wear it to the gathering." Mom ran her hand over the soft leather. "Go try it on so we can see how it fits."

Hannah ran to her bedroom, pulled off her T-shirt and shorts, and slipped the dress over her head. It hung down from her shoulders in a straight line right down to several inches below her knees. It felt heavy and warm, but she didn't care. She twisted back and forth, making the fringe flip around her legs. She tied the beaded belt around her slender waist and hung the colored beads around her neck. They almost touched the belt. She stood in front of the full-length mirror on the closet door and gasped.

"I look beautiful!" she whispered in amazement. "I always thought I was ugly!"

She ran downstairs to show Mom.

"Hannah! Oh, Hannah!" Mom walked around and around Hannah, taking in every angle. "Wait'll your dad sees you."

Hannah pressed her hand to her racing heart. "Some of the other granddaughters will be angry they didn't get the dress."

"I know," Mom said sadly. "But Great-grandma has her own mind, and she said she knew you were to have it."

"Can I show it to the Best Friends?"

"Oh, I don't know. You can't let anything happen to it. We want it in the family for years to come."

"I'll be very *very* careful."

Mom smiled as she sat back in her rocker. "Go show them, but don't stay too long . . . And don't let pride enter your heart."

Hannah spun around and laughed. It was too late. Pride was already all over her. She ran outdoors and called for her sisters to look at her dress. She stepped into the shade to keep from sweating in the hot sun as they admired the dress.

"I want one just like it," the twins said together.

"It's prettier than Cinderella's dress," Lena said in awe as she gingerly touched the fringe and the beads. "When I'm big enough can I have it?"

"You'll have to ask Great-grandma." Hannah

twirled around to make the fringe flip, then dashed across the street to Chelsea's house. She was sure Roxie and Kathy would still be there. She saw some movement in Roxie's yard and ran through Chelsea's yard on to Roxie's. The girls were looking at the flowers that had just bloomed in the flower beds Chelsea had been tending.

"Look, girls!" cried Hannah with her arms out and her head high.

They turned and gasped in admiration, then ran to Hannah, all talking at once.

"It belonged to my great-grandmother. She had to replace a few beads on the belt, but otherwise it's original."

"Show my mom," Roxie said as she gently touched the leather. "She'd love to see the crafts-manship."

"It should be hanging in a museum," Kathy added with her hands clasped at her throat.

"How will you keep it clean if you wear it to your family picnic?" Chelsea asked.

"I won't wear it the entire day, and I'll be very careful when I do have it on." Hannah pushed her dark hair back. Sweat moistened her skin from the warm dress. "I told Mom I wouldn't stay long. See you girls in the morning. I already bought the card for Ezra and the stuff for his cake."

"My mom said she'd decorate it," Roxie announced.

"See you in the morning," Chelsea said.

"We love your dress." Kathy carefully touched the beadwork. "I'm glad you showed it to us."

Hannah smiled, then ran back across the street. The twins and Lena weren't in the front yard now. A squirrel chattered as he sat in a tree near the curb.

In the house Hannah heard the girls in the kitchen with Mom. They were begging her for dresses just like Hannah's. The smell of a freshly baked cake floated out the door. Hannah tiptoed past the kitchen door and slipped upstairs. She looked in the mirror again, turning this way and that. With a long sigh she took the dress and beads off and put them carefully away. She set the box on the top shelf in the closet—out of reach of the little girls.

Dressed once again in her shorts and T-shirt she looked in the mirror, made a face, and ran downstairs. She was cooler but no longer beautiful. Just as she turned toward the kitchen the front doorbell rang. She ran to answer it, and her heart dropped to her feet.

Ginny Shigwam stood there with two suitcases beside her and a smug look on her broad face. She wore too-tight jeans, a short white blouse with red beads, and red dangling earrings. "Hi," she said, then turned and waved to a woman in a car. "A friend dropped me off."

Hannah finally was able to speak. "Come in. I thought you weren't going to be here until tomorrow night."

Ginny shrugged. "I had a chance to come now." She pushed a suitcase at Hannah. "Carry this for me. It's heavy."

Hannah turned toward the kitchen and called, "Mom, Ginny's here."

Mom rushed to the front door with the twins and Lena close behind. "Ginny! But I understood you were coming tomorrow."

"Well, I'm here . . . And I'm tired."

Hannah's jaw tightened. She couldn't remember Ginny ever being nice to anyone. "I'll take her upstairs, Mom."

"Thank you, Hannah." Mom suddenly looked too weary to stand.

"I don't remember you, Ginny," Lena said as she fell into step beside Ginny.

"I do," Vivian said, pushing up close to Ginny.

"No, you don't," Sherry said, shaking her head.

Hannah frowned at the twins. They were dressed in pink shorts and shirts and looked exactly alike. But they didn't act alike. Vivian was noisy and talked a lot. Sherry was usually quiet and liked to draw and color.

Hannah set the suitcase inside her bedroom. She'd sleep with Lena and give her bed to Ginny.

"I wish my room was this big," Ginny said as she looked around.

"It's big, but it'll be crowded with three of us." Hannah leaned against the square table and put her hands on the table. Mom had said she'd wait until Ginny left to make the twins' room a nursery. "You'll have to keep your stuff picked up and the bed made."

Ginny shrugged as she dropped a suitcase on Hannah's bed, then opened it. She lifted everything out, dropped it on the bed, closed the suitcase with a snap, then pushed it under the bed. "Which drawer can I have?"

Hannah bit back a groan as she walked over to the dresser. "This top one should be big enough." Hannah took her things out and put them in the next drawer down, filling the drawer almost too full to close. The money pouch dropped to the floor.

"Is that your piggy bank?" Ginny asked in disdain, giggling.

"No. I'm the treasurer for a group called *King's Kids*. The money belongs to them." Hannah stuffed it in the drawer and forced the drawer shut.

Ginny kicked off her sandals and started filling the top drawer with her clothes. "Who are the *King's Kids*, and who is the king?"

"I'll tell her," Lena said eagerly. "Jesus is the King. And the kids are some kids who work for other people to make extra money. Someday I'm going to be a *King's Kid*!"

"Me too," the twins said, nodding hard.

"Don't let Grandpa hear you talk about Jesus," Ginny said with a wicked chuckle. "He says the white man's Jesus has no place in our lives as Odawas."

Trembling, Hannah turned away. She didn't want to hear the old argument again about saying Odawa instead of Ottawa, or about Jesus not caring about Native Americans. Jesus was her Savior no matter what the old customs were and no matter who made fun of her.

Ginny hung a few things in the closet, then reached up and pulled the dress box from the shelf. "What's this?"

"Put that back!" Hannah cried, grabbing for it.

Ginny turned away and flipped the lid off. "Great-grandma's special dress!" Sparks shot from Ginny's coal-black eyes. "Why is it here?"

"Great-grandma gave it to Hannah," Lena said proudly. "But someday when it fits me I'll wear it."

Ginny flung the box to the floor. The dress and beads fell out onto the carpet. "Wait'll Dad hears this! He promised me that dress!"

Hannah carefully picked up the dress and packed it gently away. "The dress is mine, Ginny," Hannah said softly though inside she was raging. "*You* will never get it."

"Wait and see," Ginny snapped.

Hannah lifted her chin and looked Ginny square in the face. "You will never get it," she whispered as she clenched her fists at her sides.

3

Ezra Menski's Cake

Yawning tiredly, Hannah picked up the bag of groceries from the kitchen counter to take over to Chelsea's. Last night Ginny had talked long into the night. Hannah yawned again. She'd wanted to stuff a dirty sock in Ginny's mouth, but Lena had enjoyed every minute of Ginny's talk.

Mom walked into the kitchen and yawned as she poured herself a cup of coffee. "When will you be back?"

"In about two hours. After we bake the cake for Ezra we'll do the work at the Crandalls'." Saying that made her think about the white kittens at the Crandalls'. "Oh, Mom, I wish you'd let me have a kitten! They're so cute!"

"Sorry, Nanna."

Hannah smiled at Mom's pet name for her. It had been a long time since she'd called her that.

"I couldn't handle a kitten in my life right now . . . But maybe someday."

Hannah kissed Mom's cheek and walked outdoors. It was still early, but all the *King's Kids* started to work early. Hannah yawned again. Sometimes it was hard to get up, especially since it was summer vacation. Once school started, there'd be no sleeping in even if she wanted to.

A few minutes later she unloaded the bag of groceries on the counter in Chelsea's kitchen while the Best Friends talked about their plans for the day. The room smelled like oranges and toast.

"You won't believe who came yesterday after I saw you," Hannah said. She waited until she had their undivided attention. "Ginny!"

"No!" they cried all at once.

Hannah rolled her eyes and nodded.

"Where is she?" Roxie asked.

"Still asleep! She talked until 2 this morning. Two! I told her a million times I had to get up early, but she didn't care. She just kept talking."

While they talked about Ginny, Chelsea pulled a bowl from the cupboard and soon had the cake mixed and in the oven. Roxie and Kathy cleaned up the mess and washed the few dishes they'd used. Hannah dried them and put them away.

"I have a terrible feeling she's going to be a bad influence on Lena." Hannah frowned as she hung up the dish towel. "Oh, I can't stand to think about and talk about Ginny anymore. Let's change the subject to something fun!"

"Like Brody," Kathy said, wrinkling her nose. "He came for breakfast this morning! I was still in my pajamas! When I saw him coming to the door I raced to my room and got dressed, and when I got back to the table my cornflakes were soggy. It made me so mad!"

"I like soggy cornflakes," Roxie said.

"I think Brody's cute." Chelsea blushed and giggled.

Hannah nudged Chelsea. "I thought you liked Nick."

"He's all right, but he spends most of his time with Rob talking about computers." Chelsea sighed. "I get tired of that."

"Brody only talks about guitar and Dad." Kathy shook her head. "I know he's good at guitar, but I wish he'd learn to talk about something else."

"Did you hear any more about his brother Cole?" Hannah asked.

"He's going to be in jail a long time." Kathy shuddered. "Think of that! Wouldn't it be awful to have your own brother in jail?"

Hannah leaned on the counter. "When I was a little girl my dad was arrested." She gasped, and her pulse raced. "Oh, I wasn't supposed to tell that!"

Chelsea patted Hannah's shoulder. "Don't worry about us. We won't tell anyone."

29

"Why was he arrested?" asked Kathy.

"Because he was near the spot where a gas station was robbed and he's Native American." Hannah lowered her voice, and her stomach knotted painfully. "Some people hate American Indians. He was arrested just because he is Ottawa; they just assumed he was guilty. He had on old jeans and a sweatshirt instead of his dress clothes. They kept him in jail overnight. He was really embarrassed . . . and mad!"

"My dad would've been too," Roxie said. "He hardly ever dresses up. But he's never been arrested or anything."

"Before my dad had his ponytail cut off he was sometimes accused of doing drugs," whispered Kathy. "But he never did them. He said musicians are accused of doing drugs a lot."

Chelsea twisted her hair around her finger. "My dad said some of the people he works with take prescribed drugs because they're under so much stress. He says he's glad he knows about God's peace so he isn't even tempted to take them."

"I would never do drugs of any kind," Hannah stated.

"Me either," Chelsea, Roxie, and Kathy said together.

Just then the timer buzzed, so Chelsea checked the cake. The smell of chocolate filled the kitchen.

"It's done." Chelsea carefully set the two pans on the counter and set the timer for ten minutes.

"I hope Ezra likes chocolate cake," Kathy said.

"He does." Hannah nodded with a smile. "I found out before I went shopping. I didn't spend more than five dollars, but I didn't think you'd care. The rest can go for other things."

Kathy lifted her hand. "I have a great idea! There's a family near us—the Lawsons—and they have a new baby. Mr. Lawson is out of work for a while, and they don't have much for the baby. Let's buy formula or something for them, okay?"

"Let's vote," Chelsea said. "All in favor?" She lifted her hand at the same time the others did.

"I'll buy disposable diapers instead of formula," Hannah told them. "Mom nurses Burke, and Mrs. Lawson might do the same."

Kathy nodded. "I think she does."

"Mom will know what kind of diapers are the best," Hannah said.

They talked about babies a while. Then Chelsea said, "As soon as the timer goes off and I take the cake out of the pans we can go to the Crandalls' to work."

"Were you ever able to tell them about their white cat having kittens?" Roxie asked.

"Yes. They want us to find homes for the kittens." Chelsea sighed. "I want one, but Dad says no."

"So did my mom." Hannah shook her head. "I wish I could keep one. If Mom could see how cute they are, she might change her mind."

"I have it!" Roxie spun around with a laugh. "We'll take the kittens in their basket to our homes and show them off. Who could turn them away then?"

The girls laughed, then talked about what their families would say.

The timer buzzed, and Chelsea turned each layer onto a plate to finish cooling.

Just as Hannah led the way to the back door someone knocked. Chelsea opened the door, and Ginny walked in without even being invited. Hannah saw Ginny was wearing the shorts she'd bought just last week with her *King's Kids* pay. Anger rushed through her, but she didn't say anything.

Ginny flipped her hair back. "Hi, Hannah. Your mom said you'd be here."

"Girls, this is my cousin Ginny." Hannah introduced the girls to Ginny as they slowly walked back into the kitchen.

Ginny spied the cakes on the counter and quickly reached out and broke a piece off. "You don't mind, do you?" She ate it before anyone could stop her.

Hannah's head spun with anger and embarrassment.

"That was a birthday cake for someone," Chelsea said stiffly.

"Oh. I didn't know." Ginny shrugged and broke off another piece and ate it. "It's good."

Hannah grabbed Ginny's arm and jerked her away from the counter. "You can't eat that!"

Ginny pried Hannah's fingers loose and flung her hand away. "Don't tell me what I can or can't do! You're not my boss!"

Hannah looked helplessly at her friends. She could see they didn't know what to do either.

Roxie finally stepped up to Ginny. "We have work to do. You go back to Hannah's where you belong."

"Who's gonna make me?"

"I will!" Roxie pushed her nose almost against Ginny's. "You don't scare me. Get out of here now!"

Ginny flipped back her hair and stalked out.

Hannah bit her lip as she stared helplessly down at the cake. Inside she was yelling and throwing things, but she couldn't let her friends see her terrible anger.

"What'll we do about the cake?" Chelsea asked in a small voice.

Roxie leaned down and looked more closely at the cake. "I see a dog in it!"

"What?" the others cried.

Roxie giggled. "Not a real dog, silly. I mean I could make a dog that looks just like Gracie. Mom can frost it and put a collar on it and everything."

Chelsea nodded and laughed in delight. "Great idea!"

Hannah managed to smile, but inside she was seething at what Ginny had done.

Roxie took a sharp knife and cut the two lay-ers, laying them out on a glass tray. Soon she had a chocolate cake shaped just like Gracie. "We'll take it over to Mom and let her do what she can."

"I'm so sorry for what Ginny did," Hannah whispered around a lump in her throat.

Kathy clasped Hannah's shoulders and shook her slightly. "It's not *your* fault!"

"Quit blaming yourself," Chelsea said.

Roxie started toward the door. "You can't help what your cousin did. Now, let's go."

Hannah walked outdoors with the others, but she couldn't join in as they talked and laughed. She wanted to go home and tell Mom what Ginny had done so they'd send her home where she belonged.

Hannah glanced across the street. Ginny and Lena were perched on top of the rock. Hannah pressed her lips tightly together. Mom and Dad had forbidden anyone to climb onto the rock, so they wouldn't fall off and hurt themselves. Lena could not have climbed up on it without Ginny's help.

"Lena!" Hannah shouted. "Get down from there!"

"You can't make her!" Ginny called back.

"You can't make me!" Lena cried, waving her arms high above her head.

Hannah turned abruptly away and ran after her friends. With Ginny around, the next few days were sure to be full of trouble.

4

The B-day Party

Hannah held the birthday card as she waited on Ezra Menski's porch beside Kathy. Roxie stood just ahead of them holding the cake proudly as Chelsea knocked on the door. It was 10 in the morning, but Hannah knew Ezra would be up.

Ezra jerked the door open, thumped his cane hard, and snapped, "I didn't hire you to work today. It's Independence Day, you know. What do you want?"

"Happy birthday!" they all shouted at the same time.

Hannah managed to smile even though she was still angry at what Ginny had done to the cake yesterday.

Ezra flushed. Behind him Gracie barked. "Well, I never." He shook his head. His dark pants hung loose on his lean frame and were held up with wide green suspenders. His blue shirt was buttoned all the

35

way to his chin. He backed up a bit. "Come on in. I didn't think anyone knew about my birthday. Only one granddaughter remembered to send a card."

"I want to set this in the kitchen," Roxie said, lifting the tray higher.

Hannah remembered when Roxie had done Ezra's dishes and he'd thought she'd broken a cup and stolen a hundred dollar bill. Of course she hadn't. None of the *King's Kids* stole. It was a sin. Roxie was still hesitant about being around Ezra though.

Roxie set the covered cake on the kitchen table, whipped off the cover, and cried, "Ta da!"

"Happy birthday!" shouted the girls again.

Ezra stepped back, looking totally shocked. "What is this?" he asked weakly. "You didn't make that for me, did you?"

"Sure we did." Hannah took his arm. "Come close and look at it." She felt him tremble and saw sudden tears dampen his eyes.

He peered down at the cake. "It's Gracie! I'll be! It's Gracie!"

"And here's a card." Hannah smiled as she held it out to him.

His large bony hand trembled as he took the card. Awkwardly he opened the envelope and pulled the card out. The front page showed a dog just like Gracie chewing on an old bedroom slipper. Ezra shook his head as he studied the picture. He opened

36

the card and read the birthday greeting. "Now why did you girls go and do all this?"

"We wanted to," Kathy said softly.

"It's your birthday." Hannah patted his arm. "We wanted you to know we were thinking about you."

"Now, that's nice. Very nice."

Just then the doorbell rang. Ezra brushed at his eyes, then rubbed a hand down his shallow cheek.

"I'll answer it for you if you want," Hannah said.

"Yes . . . please do." Ezra sank to a kitchen chair and waved for the girls to sit down.

Hannah hurried through the spotless house and opened the door. Anger rushed through her when she saw Ginny and Lena standing there.

Ginny pushed her way right in, and Lena followed. "We came for the party," Ginny said with a toss of her long hair.

Hannah wanted to throw them both out, but she led them to the kitchen and introduced them to Ezra. He seemed pleased to have them.

"It's getting to be a regular party, isn't it?" he said. "Get out the paper plates and cut the cake. I think I have some ice cream in the freezer. Check to see if I do, Roxann."

Hannah saw Roxie's scowl as she hurried to the refrigerator and looked in the freezer compartment.

Only Roxie's grandma called her Roxann. Why had Ezra changed from Roxie to Roxann?

The doorbell rang again, and everyone laughed. Gracie barked, but stayed at Ezra's feet.

Hannah hurried through the house again. Would she find the twins on the porch? Nothing would surprise her now. She pulled open the door and gasped in surprise. It was Emma Potter, Roxie's grandma! She looked very pretty, all dressed up in apricot-colored slacks and blouse with a strand of pearls around her neck. Her white hair waved away from her face. Hannah liked the delicate smell of her perfume.

"Mrs. Potter! What a surprise! Are you looking for Roxie?"

"Actually no." Mrs. Potter smiled and even blushed. She fingered her white purse. "I came to wish Ezra a happy birthday. Where is he?"

"In the kitchen." Hannah had a million questions she wanted to ask as they walked to the kitchen, but she didn't ask even one.

"Grandma!" cried Roxie, dashing to her side. "Is anything wrong? Do you need me?"

"No, Roxann. I came to see Ezra."

Roxie's smile vanished and she stumbled back, almost stepping on Lena.

Emma said hello to the others, then turned to Ezra. She smiled hesitantly and nervously fingered her pearls.

Ezra stood up slowly. "Hello, Emma. I thought you weren't coming."

Emma lifted her chin. "I changed my mind."

"So you did."

"And I'm glad I did. I wouldn't want to miss the party." She looked at the cake, then turned to Roxie. "I see your hand in this, Roxann. It's wonderful!"

Hannah felt the tension in the air and wondered about it. The kitchen felt crowded and hot all at once. Didn't Roxie want her grandma to be friends with Ezra? He could be very nice when he wanted to be.

"I know your work, Roxann," Grandma Potter added.

Roxie shrugged.

"It tastes good too," Ginny said.

Hannah scowled at Ginny. Ginny lifted her chin high, then whispered something to Lena that made her giggle.

"Let's cut the cake," Ezra said with a chuckle. "I think I'm going to enjoy this birthday after all." He took Emma's hand and sat her in his chair. "Do you want coffee or tea?"

"Tea would be fine." Emma gently tugged on her hand, and Ezra let it go.

Roxie grabbed a cup from the cupboard and set it down hard on the table.

Hannah glanced at her watch. It was almost

time to go to the park for the family gathering. "I didn't know it was so late. Ginny, Lena, and I must leave. I hope you have a wonderful birthday, Ezra."

"Thank you, Hannah."

"I can stay," Ginny announced with her head held high.

"Me too," Lena said, copying Ginny.

Hannah gripped Lena's arm and frowned at her. "We're going right now. Mom said so."

Lena sighed and nodded obediently.

After many good-byes and well-wishings for the 4th, Hannah walked outdoors. Lena and Ginny followed her. The sun was hot and the sky bright blue with fluffy white clouds.

"I wanted a piece of cake," Lena said in a whiny voice.

"You'll have cake at the picnic," snapped Hannah. She didn't have any patience for Lena when she acted like this.

"I don't even want to go," Ginny said.

Lena ran ahead of Hannah, then walked backwards and looked up at her defiantly. "I am not going to wear any of my Indian clothes today."

Hannah shot a look at Ginny's smug face. This was her doing! Hannah turned back to Lena as they walked into their yard. "You'll wear what Mom says to wear!"

"I don't have to! I am tired of being Native

American! I don't like being an Indian! I want to be a plain old American like everyone else. So there!"

Hannah clamped her jaw tight to keep from yelling at Lena. Every year Ginny said that very same thing. Now she'd gotten Lena to say it. Hannah shook her finger at Lena. "Tell Dad what you just told me, Lena Shigwam!"

"I will!"

Ginny laughed as she kicked a ball one of the twins had left in the yard. "What can he do? Beat her?"

"Dad doesn't beat us!" Hannah sometimes wondered if Uncle Jonas beat Ginny; other times she wished he would.

"He spanks us," Lena said angrily. "And that's not fair!"

"If you wouldn't get naughty, he wouldn't have to spank you." Hannah knew Dad had spanked Lena for climbing on the rock. Secretly Hannah had been glad and thought Lena deserved it. She glanced at her watch again. "We have to hurry." Mom had said she'd need help loading the food in the station wagon. It was already sitting outside the garage with the back door open.

Hannah ran to the kitchen and helped Mom, then hurried to her room to put on the special dress. She lifted it down and looked at it, then frowned. It wasn't folded neatly like she'd left it. "Ginny probably tried it on," Hannah muttered as she angrily spread it out on the bed and laid out the belt and the beads beside it. She'd wear the dress now and take it off later for the games. The family loved playing games and having races.

Quickly she packed shorts, a yellow T-shirt, and sneakers in a roll bag, then slipped on the dress. She looked so beautiful! She glanced down at her sandals and frowned. No one wore moccasins to the family gatherings, but today she wished she had a pair to go with her wonderful dress.

Vivian stuck her head into the room. She wore a dress similar to Hannah's and had a beaded band around her forehead. "Momma said it's time to go."

"I'm ready." Hannah smiled at Vivian. "You look very pretty, Viv."

"Thanks." Vivian touched Hannah's fringe on her sleeve. "You do too. Ginny's mad. Did you know that?"

"Yes. I wish she wasn't."

Vivian slipped her hand into Hannah's as they walked down the hall to the stairs. "She made Lena say bad things to me and Sherry. Momma slapped her mouth. And Lena cried."

"That's too bad." Hannah sighed and shook her head. "You and Sherry should let Lena hang around with you today so she stays away from Ginny. Ginny's bad for her."

"I know. She's bad for me and Sherry too. We

even said a bad word." Vivian's coal-black eyes widened. "It was terrible!"

"Just don't do the bad things she wants you to do, Viv."

"I won't. And Sherry won't either." Vivian ran out the door calling to Sherry.

Her roll bag in her hand, Hannah walked across the grass to the station wagon. She saw Dad close the back door and turn to face her. He pushed his cowboy hat to the back of his head and rested his hands on his hips. He wore jeans, a wide belt with a big buckle, and cowboy boots.

"Look at you!" Dad said with a whistle.

Hannah laughed breathlessly and lifted her chin higher as she slowly turned to show Dad the dress from every angle.

"You are Odawa!" He stretched out the three syllables and stressed the O and the *da* just like Grandpa Shigwam always did.

Hannah giggled. Just then she glanced at the station wagon. Ginny was glaring at her from the backseat. Hannah looked quickly away and walked to the car. She would not let Ginny ruin this very special 4th of July!

5

The Family Gathering

Hannah carried a covered apple pie toward the rows of tables the family had reserved. Every 4th of July the Shigwam family got together. Some came from as far away as the Upper Peninsula. That made Hannah smile as she remembered the day Chelsea had learned Michigan was two peninsulas—a lower one where they lived and an upper one that was on the other side of the Mackinac Bridge. Chelsea had come from Oklahoma with states on every side instead of water.

The park seemed full of Ottawas gathered in clumps here and there. Their cars, pickups, and station wagons or vans nearly filled the parking area where Hannah's dad had parked.

"Chief!" shouted a couple of Dad's cousins.

Hannah set the pie on the table and watched the men talk to Dad. Almost everyone called him Chief. Grandpa thought it was degrading, but Dad laughed and said it was only a nickname. Years ago as a teenager he'd gotten tired of correcting people and had accepted the nickname. But Grandpa wouldn't. Grandpa was proud of his heritage. He could name his ancestors all the way back to the eighteenth century, even though at that time the men had several wives and a lot of children. Grandpa listed them off as often as anyone would listen.

The women crowded around Hannah to look at her dress. Most of them had on clothes they wore to powwows, while others dressed in jeans or shorts. They all wore long colored earrings and beads.

Aunt Marge, Ginny's mother, scowled at Hannah and shook her finger. "Ginny was to have that dress."

Hannah swallowed hard. She looked helplessly at Mom, who sat on the bench nursing baby Burke.

"No, Marge," Hannah's mom said. "Great-grandma gave it to Hannah. Talk to Chief if you have a problem with that."

"I will have Jonas talk to him! They are brothers!" Aunt Marge turned away in anger and stalked off toward Uncle Jonas. He was playing horseshoe with three other men. To Hannah's relief Uncle Jonas kept on playing.

Hannah backed away while the women tried to comfort her mom. They all knew what a sharp tongue Aunt Marge had. Hannah looked across the park and wished the Best Friends would suddenly turn up. But she knew they all had plans for the day with their own families. She looked longingly toward the path that led to Betina Quinn's estate. Betina would enjoy seeing her. Probably Betina and Lee Malcomb and his foster kids Mark and Allie were having a picnic together. Hannah hoped Betina and Lee would get married. So did the other Best Friends.

Slowly Hannah walked over to a group of girls her age near the swings. Most of the girls were her cousins. Others were related somehow, but she wasn't sure exactly how. Most of them wore dresses similar to hers and beaded bands around their foreheads. A few of them looked more white than Ottawa. That was because they were part white and part Ottawa.

Hannah stopped beside Betty, one of her favorite cousins. She wore red shorts and a white T-shirt. Long beaded earrings dangled to her slender shoulders. "Hi," Hannah said, smiling.

"Hi, Hannah. The dress is beautiful on you. I'm glad Great-grandma gave it to you." Betty leaned toward Hannah and giggled. "My sisters and I were afraid she'd give it to Ginny even if she hates being Odawa."

Another cousin, Linda, touched Hannah's arm. "My mother once wore this dress when she was twelve. She had her picture taken with it on. The photo is framed and hangs in her bedroom now. She was very pretty."

With shouting and laughing going on all around them, the girls talked about school and boys and what they planned to do the rest of the summer. Hannah was glad Ginny stayed away. Twice she saw Ginny with Lena, and she frowned. She thought of telling Mom what a bad influence Ginny was on Lena, but she didn't.

Just before the picnic lunch the boys and girls sang and danced for the adults. Grandpa quizzed them on Odawa words. He didn't want the language to die. The men told stories of the past. The old men told stories of their ancestors. Hannah's grandpa said it was very important for all of them to know their history. Some of the stories were interesting, and others bored Hannah, but she tried not to let it show when she wasn't interested. She didn't want to bring shame on her father in front of his family.

Hannah's stomach growled, and she looked hungrily at the tables sagging with food. Finally her grandma shouted that it was time to eat. Her grandma looked different from Roxie's. She was short and heavy with thick gray hair. She was fun to talk to because she always had a funny story to tell about what had happened to her sometime in her life. And her stories were always new. She wasn't like Grandpa—his stories were always the same.

Just as everyone started to line up to fill their paper plates, Great-grandma came. She had been too weak to come for the entire day. She wore a plaid cotton dress almost to her ankles that hung loose over her thin body. Her white hair was pulled back in three rolls and pinned to her round head. She greeted everyone who ran up to her by name. She was proud of her sharp mind. Hannah hung back until there was an opening, then slowly walked over to Great-grandma.

"Thank you for the dress, Great-grandma."

Great-grandma looked Hannah up and down with her weak black eyes. "It suits you as I knew it would. Now get out of my way and let me eat."

Hannah smiled and stepped back. Great-grandma had a soft heart but a sharp tongue.

Two uncles seated Great-grandma at an empty table with a red plaid plastic tablecloth while an aunt filled her plate with the foods she said she wanted. She always wanted her plate heaping full, then couldn't eat more than a third of it. She'd have them pack the rest for her to take home. She lived about fifty miles away and had asked one of her grandsons to drive her here.

The smells of fried chicken, fresh bread, baked beans, and coffee made Hannah's mouth water. There were vegetables, salads, pickles, and desserts galore, and drinks of every kind. She knew she'd take red punch. It was her favorite. Some of the men had brought cans of beer, but she knew Dad wouldn't drink any.

Finally Hannah was next in line. She picked up a thick paper plate, a white napkin, and a plastic fork, knife, and spoon. She'd fill her plate, then get her punch. The punch was in a huge turquoise cooler on a table that held only drinks, a chest of ice, and paper cups.

A firecracker popped, and Hannah jumped. Several boys laughed and lit a few more. The bangs were loud despite the voices of the people around the tables. It was illegal to buy or sell firecrackers in Michigan, but someone always had them anyway and fired them off just for the fun of startling everyone. Hannah knew Cousin Lyle brought fireworks every year, even though he was told not to. Two years ago Hannah had lit a firecracker, and it had almost blown up in her fingers before she could throw it down. She'd been afraid to try again.

Hannah took a crispy fried chicken breast, potato chips, three dill pickles, two carrot sticks, a red salad she'd liked last year that Aunt Marge always brought, some macaroni salad, and a large brownie with nuts and chocolate frosting. Somewhere behind her in the line she heard Ginny laughing and talking to Cousin Ted. Ginny flirted with anyone she could, even if he was a cousin. Hannah hated to think of Ginny meeting Chelsea's brother Rob and Kathy's brother Duke.

Forcing away thoughts of Ginny, Hannah picked up a tall glass of red punch and carefully walked over to a table where other cousins were sitting. Her mouth was dry, and she wanted to drain her glass, but she knew she had to be very careful of her dress. She should've changed after Great-grandma saw her and before she ate. She shrugged. Her plate was full, and besides she was too hungry to change right now. It wouldn't hurt to wait a few minutes more. She smiled at her cousins and sat down carefully. She sighed with bliss as she picked up her glass of punch and drank. It was every bit as good as she thought it would be. She talked and laughed with her cousins as she ate everything she'd taken. The dill pickles made her pucker up, but she liked them anyway.

Just then she heard the twins laugh. She looked at the table where the little kids sat. The twins were enjoying all the cousins their age. Hannah looked for Lena, but couldn't see her. Finally she found her sitting under a tree with Ginny. Hannah frowned. Should she get Lena and take her to the cousins her age? Hannah shrugged. Why bother? Lena was determined to hang around Ginny.

Across the park some of the boys played with a Frisbee, while others played softball. All the picnic tables in the park were full of people eating. A warm breeze blew smells of barbecued ribs and grilled steaks over from a smoking grill. A blonde girl walked past with a tape player blasting rock 'n' roll.

Betty began telling about her sister's coming wedding. She was marrying a second cousin. Betty lowered her voice. "Dad was afraid she'd marry the white boy she went out with last year."

Hannah picked absently at the red plaid table-cloth. Would she marry an Ottawa someday? What would Mom and Dad say if she married a white man? She glanced at the two white women who'd married Ottawa men. Everyone loved and accepted them . . . or did they?

Abruptly Hannah swung around on the bench and carried her paper cup to get a refill. She was debating about filling her plate again. There were several desserts she wanted to try. And the grilled burgers sure smelled good.

She dropped two partly melted ice cubes into her glass, then filled it with punch. Slowly she walked away from the table, sipping her drink and watching and listening to the others. On normal days she sometimes thought her family was the only Native Americans alive. But when she went to a family gathering and saw all the others related to her, it felt good to know they weren't alone. She listened eagerly to the many more not related by blood.

"Having fun, Hannah?" Ginny asked with a smirk.

Hannah nodded as she stiffened, her punch almost at her lips.

"I'm glad. I can make it even better." Ginny reached out and bumped Hannah's hand, then laughed as she dashed away.

In slow motion the red punch bounced out of the glass and splashed down the front of the special dress that had been in the family for years.

Hannah cried out and tried to jump back out of the way, but she was too slow. The damage had already been done. Frantically she ran for a napkin and tried to blot the red punch off the dress. A dark stain covered the front of her dress around the beadwork and down past her waist.

"Hannah, what have you done?" Great-grandma cried, shaking a thin finger at Hannah. "Burke, see what your daughter has done to my dress!"

Mom quickly handed the baby to an aunt and ran to Hannah just as Dad did the same. They both pressed at the stain with napkins.

"What happened?" Dad asked quietly.

"I told you to be careful," Mom said impatiently.

Tears welled up in Hannah's eyes. She tried to speak, but couldn't without bursting into tears. She would not cry in front of everyone!

"Don't worry about it," Dad said gently. "It's only a dress. We'll see that the stain is removed."

Hannah leaned thankfully against Dad with her face pressed into his arm. She couldn't stand to see all the accusing faces around her. She knew everyone blamed her for being careless. Probably no one had seen Ginny bump her glass. It had happened too quickly.

"Go change your clothes," Mom said, patting Hannah's shoulder. "What's done is done."

"Is the dress ruined?" called Great-grandma.

"No," Dad said. He gently pushed Hannah away and whispered, "Run and change. Remember, Jesus is with you. I'll take care of Great-grandma and the others."

Hannah walked away as the cousins called out to her. She broke into a run and ran to the station wagon that seemed to be ten miles away. She grabbed her roll bag while tears poured down her flushed cheeks. Weakly she leaned against the station wagon and struggled to control her sobs. The sun burned down on her, but she didn't notice.

Finally she pulled herself together enough to walk to the brick building where the restroom was. Thankfully it was empty. The smell turned her stomach as she pulled on her shorts and T-shirt. She caught a glimpse of her reflection in the mirror and scowled. Oh, but she looked ugly! With a strangled sob she carefully folded the dress and stuck it in the bag with the beads and the belt. "Jesus, I really really need Your help," she whispered.

Taking a deep breath Hannah hurried to the station wagon, set the bag in the back, then slowly walked across the park to the family gathering. She caught sight of Ginny sitting on a swing next to Lena.

"That is the last time you're going to be mean to me, Ginny Shigwam," Hannah muttered with her fists clenched at her sides.

6

Getting Even

Hannah trembled as she drew closer to the group of cousins. It felt like a million eyes were on her, all accusing her of ruining the special dress.

Betty stepped forward and slipped her hand through Hannah's arm. "We don't blame you," she whispered. "Angela saw what Ginny did."

"Did she tell Great-grandma?"

"Oh, no! Ginny would do something terrible to Angela if she did." Betty led Hannah into the center of the cluster of cousins. "I told Hannah," Betty said to the other cousins.

"I hear Ginny's staying at your house a while," Hilery said, shaking her head and sending her long earrings swaying.

Hannah nodded. "We don't know for how long yet."

"I wonder what it is this time?" Patty asked, giggling. "When she stayed with us it was because she was hanging around a sixteen-year-old white boy." Everyone laughed.

Sarah tapped her chest. "When Uncle Jonas sent her to stay with us, it was because she was failing fourth grade. Mom helped her with her reading, and Ginny managed to pass by the skin of her teeth."

"Why is she at your house, Hannah?" Sue asked in a hushed voice.

"I don't know really."

"Has she been drinking?"

Hannah locked her fingers together. Here was her chance! She shrugged as she tried to think just how she'd say Ginny was drinking when she had no idea if she really was.

"I bet that's it," Betty said, nodding. "I know Uncle Jonas and Aunt Marge drink a lot. But they don't want Ginny to start since they've been trying to quit."

"That is it, isn't it, Hannah?" Patty jabbed Hannah's arm. "Isn't that it?"

Hannah shrugged again. "Well, maybe. I'm not supposed to say." There! She hadn't really told a lie.

"I knew it!" Patty turned to the others. "I knew it was drinking!"

Hannah stood quietly as the story of Ginny's drinking problem grew bigger and bigger until it was an absolute fact that she was usually in a state of drunken stupor and was seldom sober.

"Your dad and mom should be able to help her

since they don't believe in drinking," Betty said. She grinned sheepishly. "I wouldn't be so nice. I'd see that she got all the beer or whiskey she wanted just to get even."

The cousins giggled, and Hannah tried to, but couldn't manage it. Her stomach knotted painfully.

Angela gasped, her hands on her cheeks. "Hannah, what if she gets Lena to drinking?"

Hannah shook her head. "No! I wouldn't let her!"

"Lena hangs on Ginny and does everything she says," Sarah said. "I've watched her today. If Ginny gave Lena beer, she'd drink it."

"I hope your dad watches her close. It would be awful for a nine-year-old to become an alcoholic."

They all talked about that for a while. Some of them told about drinking beer and liking it, while others said they'd tasted it and hated it. Hannah had only smelled beer, and she hated even the smell. None of them wanted to get dependent on it.

"Let's go play kickball or something," Hannah suggested so they'd quit talking about Ginny and Lena and drinking. "We brought a kickball." It was one of her favorite games, and she was good at it.

"Yeah! Kickball!" Betty shouted. "You get the ball, and we'll find the spot to play."

Hannah ran toward the tree where they'd left the balls and bats and other games. From the corner of her eye she saw Ginny walk around some bushes with what looked like a can of beer in her hand. Had they been right about her? Hannah's pulse leaped as she sneaked over to get a closer look. Maybe it was only a can of pop.

Her heart hammering, Hannah ducked around the bushes. Ginny stood a few feet away with the can to her lips. It *was* beer! Suddenly Hannah saw her chance to get even. She leaped forward and bumped Ginny. The beer can tipped, and beer spilled down Ginny's chin onto her blouse. The smell was terrible!

"Look what you did!" screamed Ginny, her face dark with rage.

Hannah trembled, but she forced out a laugh. "I'll take you to your mom and dad and let them clean you up."

Ginny rubbed at her chin and her blouse. "You think you're smart, don't you?"

"You're not supposed to drink!"

"It's for my dad."

"Oh, sure." Hannah grinned. It probably was for Uncle Jonas, but she wouldn't let Ginny see she believed her.

"I'm telling my dad I want to go home with him today."

"Good!"

Ginny trembled. "You want to get rid of me, don't you? Well, that's just too bad."

"Your dad sent you to us, and he won't take you

home even if you beg him. What trouble did you get in this time, Ginny Shigwam? Just how bad is it?"

"I hate you!"

"So what else is new?"

Ginny hurried away, and Hannah ran after her.

"Somebody bring Ginny a napkin," Hannah called, laughing in her head, but heavy in her heart. "She spilled her drink on her."

Aunt Trudy ran to Ginny and dabbed at her blouse, then frowned. "Ginny, you've been drinking!"

Hannah hid a grin, while Ginny sputtered with anger.

Aunt Trudy turned and called to the table of women, "This child has been drinking beer!"

"She was only taking it to her father," Aunt Marge said quickly as she ran to Ginny. "Let me have it. I'll take it to him."

Ginny glared at Hannah, then reluctantly went with Aunt Trudy to change her blouse.

Hannah turned away and almost ran into Lena. She'd changed into her red shorts and white T-shirt with red balloons on it.

"What did you do to her?" Lena asked sharply, her fists doubled at her sides.

Hannah pushed her face close to Lena's. "I caught her drinking beer. Don't you dare try to copy her!"

Lena lifted her chin high. "I don't copy her!"

"You've been copying her ever since she got here!"

"You're just jealous because she likes me and hates you!"

Hannah jabbed Lena's arm. "Take that back."

"No!" Lena shook her head hard, and her dark braids flipped over her thin shoulders. "You're not my boss."

Hannah wanted to shake Lena, but she forced her anger back. She took a deep breath. "I'm sorry, Lena. I'm on my way to get the kickball. Want to play with us?"

Lena nodded, then frowned. "Is Ginny playing?"

"I doubt it. She doesn't like to."

"Then I won't!"

"See, you are a copycat!"

Lena turned on her heels and raced away, her thin legs pumping up and down, her sneakers barely touching the grass.

Sighing heavily, Hannah ran to the tree and picked up the kickball. Why hadn't she kept her big mouth shut? She shouldn't have called Lena a copycat. Now she'd copy Ginny all the more.

Hannah ran across the park and tossed the ball to Sarah. Sarah said she was the pitcher for her team. She and Angela had already picked sides, and Hannah was on Angela's. Their team was up first.

"What happened with Ginny?" Betty asked. "We heard all the commotion."

Hannah hung her head. "I don't want to say."

The cousins gathered round, begging her to tell just like she knew they would.

She lifted her head and said hesitantly, "She was drinking a can of beer, and she spilled it all over herself."

"I was right!" one cousin shouted.

"I thought for sure it was another boy she was hanging out with. But drinking!" another cousin exclaimed.

Hannah listened to her cousins' comments without saying a word. She tried to feel happy about getting even with Ginny, but she didn't feel happy at all. She knew Jesus didn't want her to get even. He wanted her to love Ginny. But that was totally impossible!

"Play ball!" Sarah shouted as she ran to the pitcher's mound.

"You're up first, Hannah," Angela said. "Kick yourself home."

Sarah rolled the ball toward home base. Hannah waited, then kicked. The ball shot into the air, and she raced for first base.

"Out!" cried Sue. "Penny caught it!"

"Too bad," Hannah's team called as Hannah slowly walked to the side to wait in line for another turn, her face red with embarrassment. The first out and she'd made it! She didn't get a chance to be up again before the third out. She ran to the field while Sarah's team ran in.

Just then Ginny shouted, "We want to play. Lena and me do!"

Hannah's heart sank. She saw the looks pass between different girls.

"Let 'em play," Angela called. "Lena on our team and Ginny on Sarah's."

"I'll be up first," Ginny cried as she ran to home plate.

Hannah tried to catch Lena's eye, but she wouldn't look her way. Lena stayed as far away from her as she could get. "Who cares," Hannah muttered. But she knew she *did* care. Lena might be a pest and only nine, but she was her sister.

Renea rolled the ball toward Ginny. She kicked it, and it sailed toward Lena.

"Catch it, Lena!" everyone shouted.

Lena caught it, then fumbled it, and it fell to the ground.

Hannah frowned. She'd played kickball with Lena many times, and she knew Lena was a good catcher.

"Throw it to first!" cried Angela.

Lena picked up the ball, started to throw it, then fumbled it again. Before she could get it, Ginny reached first base.

"Sorry," Lena called as she tossed the ball to Renea.

Hannah groaned. Had Lena fumbled on purpose so Ginny could get to first base? Hannah glanced at Lena just as she looked her way.

Lena giggled and brushed her hands together.

Hannah's temper flared. Lena *had* done it on purpose!

Trudy was up next. She kicked the ball, and Hannah caught it, then threw it hard at Ginny as she raced for second base. The ball missed Ginny, and she reached second safely. She stuck her tongue out at Hannah, then turned and waved at Lena.

Hannah impatiently brushed a strand of black hair off her damp cheek. The game was no longer fun. Ginny and Lena were going to try to mess up the whole game. Hannah bit her lip. Should she warn Angela?

Hannah glanced back to find Angela near second base. She edged her way to her and quickly whispered what she thought Ginny and Lena were planning.

"Thanks for telling me," Angela said in a low voice. She chuckled. "We'll take care of that fast! You play near Lena and take her catches, and I'll tell Sarah to put somebody on Ginny. We won't let them ruin the game."

Hannah laughed in relief as she dashed toward Lena, stopping behind her. The hot sun burned down on Hannah. Up above an airplane flew across the bright blue sky.

Lena glanced back with a frown. Hannah shrugged and smiled.

Just then Patty kicked the ball right toward Lena. Hannah leaped forward, bumped Lena out of the way, and caught the ball.

"Out!" Sue cried, her hands held high.

Grinning, Hannah tossed the ball to Renea.

"Let me play my own space," Lena snapped in a low voice.

"Sure. Okay." Hannah grinned as she backed away. She bent low, her hands on her knees as she watched the next girl up. It was Lucille, and she was good. Hannah tensed, ready to spring forward. But the ball sailed into left field, and she relaxed.

Suddenly Lena rammed into Hannah, sending her sprawling to the ground.

"Why'd you do that?" Hannah snapped as she jumped up and glared at Lena.

"Do what? I was going after the ball and you were in my way," Lena said innocently.

"The ball was in left field!"

"Oh. I thought it was coming this way." Lena giggled as she walked back to her place.

Hannah brushed grass and dirt off her back as she stared at Lena. She'd never been such a brat. Ginny really was a bad influence on her. Hannah pinched her lips thoughtfully. Was it too late to help Lena see what Ginny was doing to her?

7

Cousin Ansell

With the girls running ahead of her to eat again, Hannah walked away from the kickball game with her head held high. Their team had won! She glanced to her left where Ginny and Lena were walking together, whispering and giggling. Just what were they up to this time? They hadn't been able to ruin the game as they'd planned. And it had looked like they'd had fun playing once they realized they couldn't carry out their terrible plan.

"Race you to the table, Lena," Ginny shouted with a laugh.

Lena made a face at Hannah, then sped toward the table, easily overtaking Ginny.

Just as Hannah reached the wishing well someone called to her. She turned to see Cousin Ansell leaning against the well. His black hair brushed against the collar of his western shirt. He stood with his thumbs looped in his jeans. He was sixteen years old, and she was surprised he'd speak to her since she was only eleven going on twelve. She slowly walked to him and leaned against the well beside him. "Hi," she said, smiling hesitantly.

Ansell tipped his head slightly. "Hannah, I know you and Ginny don't get along."

"You're right, we don't."

"But I also know that Jesus is your personal Savior."

She nodded, surprised he'd even mention it. Usually talk of any religion was sidestepped except when Grandpa got started on their ancestors.

"You can help Ginny."

Hannah's eyes widened. "How?"

"Tell her about Jesus."

"She won't listen!"

"Tell her anyway."

"Uncle Jonas would get mad."

Ansell chewed on his bottom lip, then finally said, "Hannah, Uncle Jonas doesn't know what to do. He doesn't have a clue. But he knows your dad does because he knows Jesus. They all saw the change in your dad when he turned to Christianity when he was about my age. He stopped drinking altogether."

Hannah bit back a gasp. Dad had never told her about his life before he became a Christian. She never knew about his drinking. He even had a fit if they watched beer commercials on TV.

Ansell looked down at all the coins in the water at the bottom of the wishing well. "If wishing helped, the whole world would be perfect."

"I know."

"Ginny is becoming dependent on alcohol."

Hannah slapped her hand to her mouth. What she and her cousins had said was true! Maybe Ginny really had intended to drink the can of beer she said was for her dad!

"She started drinking seriously last year."

"How do you know?" Hannah asked hoarsely.

"I've seen her. I see her almost every day because we live near her." He turned to Hannah, his face full of agony. "I tried to get her to stop, but she only laughed at me."

Hannah frowned. "Why do you even care?"

Ansell ducked his head and turned away. In a harsh whisper he said, "I don't want her to suffer like I am."

Hannah's heart lurched. "Oh, Ansell . . ."

"I started, and I can't quit."

Her mouth felt bone-dry. "Why don't you get help?"

"I don't want anyone to know."

"Talk to my dad! He'll help you. You know he will."

"I can't expect him to take *me* in too."

She plucked at his sleeve. "Just talk to him!"

Ansell stabbed his fingers through his coarse

black hair. "I don't want him to know. He thinks I'm doing fine in school and plan to go on to college. But I flunked three of my classes my sophomore year. How can I even go back to school in September?"

"You're no coward, Ansell Shigwam!"

He faced her squarely. "But I am!"

Hannah shook her head hard. "No! No, you are not! You are Odawa! Proud! Important!"

"Looked down on," he said in a low harsh voice. "Called 'lazy.' Called 'no good Indian.'"

"Then prove they're wrong! Make something of yourself."

"I tried, but I can't."

"Jesus will help you!" Hannah whispered.

"I don't know Him. Grandpa says we don't need the white man's belief in Jesus."

Hannah struggled with the right words to say. She wished the Best Friends were with her. With all of them together they always had the answers. But they weren't here, and she was. And so was the Holy Spirit! Suddenly a Bible verse popped into her head. "Ansell, 'God so loved the world'—and you—'that He sent His only begotten Son Jesus, that whoever believes on Him shall not perish but shall have everlasting life.'"

"I don't know, Hannah." Ansell helplessly shook his head. "I just don't know."

"Talk to Dad!"

"I might."

"Please!"

"Maybe." He touched her shoulder. "Don't say a word about me and my . . . problem to anyone."

Hannah bit her lip. "I won't."

Ansell gripped her arms. "It might be too late for me, but it's not for Ginny. Help her all you can!"

"But I want to help *you*, and so would Dad!"

"I don't know! I'll think about it." Ansell looked into her face a long time, then strode away with his head down and his shoulders bent.

Hannah leaned weakly against the wishing well. "Help him, Jesus," she whispered with tears in her eyes. She'd always admired Ansell from a distance. He was good-looking and always seemed to be having fun. Never would she have believed he was in such trouble. Behind her, kids shouted and laughed. In a nearby tree a squirrel scolded noisily. Smells of grilled hamburgers drifted on the wind, but her hunger had disappeared.

Hannah brushed at her tears and looked down at the coins in the wishing well. Mom had told her for years that wishing couldn't change anything, that only trust and faith in God could. Mom was right. "Heavenly Father, I do trust You and believe You. Send Ansell help. Let him know Jesus loves him. Thank You, Lord."

She thought of Ginny too, but that made her think about the special dress, and that made her anger explode like a firecracker. She'd pray for

Ansell and try to help him, but not Ginny. She was too mean!

Slowly Hannah walked toward a group of cousins waiting for grilled hamburgers. She couldn't see Ginny or Lena. The twins were riding on the merry-go-round with several others their age. Lena should've been with them. The twins squealed and giggled as Uncle Ralph pushed the merry-go-round faster and faster. Hannah laughed as she remembered having fun riding the same merry-go-round even though she'd always been afraid she'd fall off.

She turned, and the laugh died on her lips when she saw Ginny standing there with her arms folded and a smug look on her face. "What?" Hannah asked cautiously.

"I am staying at your house for a whole month! And you can't make me leave."

Hannah's heart sank. A whole month! How could she put up with Ginny for an entire month? And what would happen to Lena? "Do my folks know?"

Ginny flipped back her long hair. "Of course. I heard them talking with Dad."

Hannah twisted the tail of her T-shirt around her finger. "How come you're staying? You never did say."

A frightened look crossed Ginny's face, then was gone so quickly Hannah wasn't sure what she'd seen.

"Mom and Dad are going on a trip."

"Why don't they take you along?"

Ginny didn't answer for a long time. She rubbed her hands up and down her arms. "They want to have time alone."

"How come?"

Ginny frowned. "Because they hate me, just like everybody else does!"

"That's not true and you know it!" Hannah took a step toward Ginny. Just what was the truth— what Ansell had said or what Ginny was saying now?

"Why are you looking at me like that?" snapped Ginny.

"Like what?"

"Like you know something about me."

Hannah looked past Ginny across the park. "There's Cousin Ansell. Have you talked to him today?"

Ginny whipped around. "I thought he stayed home today!"

"Why would he do that?"

"None of your business!"

"I thought you got along with him."

"Who says I don't?"

Hannah wanted to ask Ginny outright if she drank, but she knew Ginny wouldn't admit it even if it was true. "Ansell looks sad today, doesn't he?"

Ginny tossed her head impatiently. "I don't

71

know why he should. He's got everything. Even his own pickup. He's handsome. He could even pass as a dark-skinned white man."

Hannah gasped in shock. "He wouldn't want to!"

"Oh yes he would! I should know."

"Is that why he drinks?" Hannah wanted to grab back the words, but it was too late.

Ginny darted a look around. "Shhh! Somebody might hear you." Ginny narrowed her black eyes. "Who told you he does?"

Just then Hannah saw her mom wave to her. "Mom wants me." Hannah ran away from Ginny as fast as she could. Oh, how could she break her word to Ansell? But Ginny already knew, so it wasn't as if she'd told someone who didn't know.

Hannah stopped beside the bench. "Did you want me?"

Mom held Burke out to Hannah. "Please hold him a while so I can play a game of horseshoe."

"Sure." Hannah held Burke tightly against her as she sat down. His eyes were wide open, but he looked contented.

"Thanks," Mom said, smiling as she handed the burp cloth to Hannah. "He should go to sleep in a few minutes. Just lay him in his little bed, but stay with him, okay?"

"I will." Hannah rubbed her cheek against Burke's soft head as Mom walked away with the other women. Burke was adorable, even if she did have to take care of him when she really didn't want to. He smelled like baby powder. She looked up and caught sight of Ansell. Once he'd been a sweet little baby. Now he was sixteen and dependent on alcohol. How awful if such a terrible thing happened to baby Burke! "Jesus, keep him safe," whispered Hannah.

Just then the twins ran up with several cousins their age. "Is the baby awake?" asked Vivian.

"Yes." Hannah held Burke out for everyone to admire.

"He's our brother," Sherry said proudly.

"We know," Carl said. "You showed him to us twice before."

"We're proud of him." Hannah smiled at Carl, then at the twins.

"Let's go down the slide!" Vivian waved her arm high. She led the way across the park, but Sherry didn't follow.

Sherry sat on the bench beside Hannah and rested her head on Hannah's arm.

"Why aren't you going, Sherry?"

"I heard those white men talking about Indians," Sherry said in a low voice as she pointed to a group of men on the other side of the park.

Hannah's stomach knotted. She remembered all the times she'd run to Mom or Dad with the very same thing. "And?"

"They said . . ." Sherry's voice faded away.

"Yes?"

"They said, 'The only good Indian is a dead Indian.' That wasn't very nice, was it?"

Hannah moved Burke enough so she could slip an arm around Sherry. "Since we don't believe it, we don't even have to think about whether it's nice or not. God made us, just like He made all other people. We know that, and we're proud!"

Sherry smiled and nodded, then jumped down and ran to join the others at the slide.

Hannah lifted Burke to her shoulder and whispered against his cheek, "God made you, Burke. Don't you ever forget it. He made you, so be proud!"

"You hate him as much as you hate me," snapped Lena.

Hannah looked up in surprise. "I don't hate him . . . or you."

"You do too, and I know it!" Lena's eyes flashed, and she looked ready to cry. "So there!" She dashed away and disappeared behind a clump of bushes.

Hannah wanted to shout for Lena to come back, but she didn't want to frighten Burke. She sighed.

"Lena, don't believe everything Ginny tells you," Hannah whispered hoarsely.

8

Chelsea's Invitation

Hannah opened her eyes and yawned. Ginny and Lena were still asleep in Lena's bed. They'd all stayed up late last night and watched fireworks, then had strawberry cheesecake ice cream, Mom's favorite, while they watched a comedy on TV. The twins had fallen asleep on the living room floor, and Dad had carried them to bed.

With another yawn Hannah swung her feet to the floor and sat on the edge of her bed. Ginny had declared that she and Lena would sleep together since Hannah hated them both. Hannah had been too tired to argue.

She glanced at the clock. In fifteen minutes she had to meet the Best Friends at the Crandall house to work. She glanced out the window. The sky was overcast, and it looked like it might rain. She slipped on jeans and a red knit top. She pulled her hair back and held it in place with a red stretchband. She pulled her sneakers from under her bed.

A few minutes later she sat at the table over a bowl of raisin bran with banana slices in it. The house seemed extra-quiet. Dad was already at work, and Mom was probably still sleeping since the baby and the twins were. Hannah slowly chewed her cereal as she thought about yesterday. She'd wanted to talk to Dad, but couldn't find a time when he was alone. Maybe she could today when he came home. He'd want to know about Ginny. And about Ansell. Just what was the truth about Ginny? Hannah hopelessly shook her head.

Yesterday just before they'd left the park she'd seen Ansell sitting alone on a park bench. She'd run to him and whispered, "I take back my promise not to tell anyone. I'll tell my dad."

"So tell him," he'd snapped. But she'd seen relief in his eyes.

With a picture of Ansell stuck in her head, Hannah set her bowl and spoon in the sink. "I *will* tell Dad," Hannah whispered as she walked to the front door.

Outdoors the air was comfortably warm but threatened rain. It was quiet up and down Ash Street as Hannah raced down the sidewalk to the Crandalls'. Kathy's bike leaned against the porch, so Hannah knew the girls were already there. From inside dogs barked. Hannah slipped in the back door and called, "I'm here!"

"We're in with the kittens," Chelsea called from the utility room.

Hannah hurried into the room and bent over the basket of white kittens between Roxie and Kathy. Chelsea knelt at the head of the basket. "They grew again." Hannah rubbed her finger over a soft white kitten.

Roxie held one against her face and closed her eyes. "I'd call this one Cuddles if it were mine."

"How was the family reunion yesterday?" Kathy asked Hannah.

Hannah sat back on her heels. "It was okay."

"Just okay?" Chelsea asked, lifting a red eyebrow.

"*We* had a great time *fishing*," Roxie said, wrinkling her nose. "Dad's idea, of course."

"Ginny caused trouble," Hannah said. "And she's staying an entire month with us!"

"Maybe you can help her," Kathy said.

"What do you mean by that?" snapped Hannah. Then she flushed. "Sorry. I know I should want to help her, but she really *really* makes me mad. And she's making Lena do terrible things."

Everyone was quiet. The mews of the kittens sounded loud. The mother cat jumped into the basket and purred.

"I have an idea," Chelsea said softly.

"What?"

"Invite Ginny to join in with us during the month she's here."

Hannah groaned.

"I don't know if I could take having her around," Roxie said with her face still against the kitten's soft fur.

Hannah bristled. Roxie had only accepted her because of Chelsea. "Because she's Ottawa?" Hannah asked stiffly.

Roxie scowled at Hannah. "Because she's a brat. I know she's your cousin, but she is a brat."

"Roxie doesn't mean to hurt your feelings," Kathy said.

Hannah sank cross-legged to the floor. She knew what Roxie really thought about her, but she didn't want to cause an argument now.

Roxie put the kitten back in the basket. "I guess I can stand to have Ginny around if it'll help. I did promise to do good deeds."

Hannah didn't feel like she could do a good deed right now, especially where Ginny was concerned. As Best Friends they'd promised to do good deeds and to read their Bible and pray regularly. She hadn't read her Bible for three days. But she had prayed now and then.

"Shall we vote on it?" Chelsea looked at them questioningly.

"Yes." Kathy nodded.

Roxie shrugged. "I guess."

"I don't want her around," Hannah whispered, hot with embarrassment at her terrible admission.

"Then we won't invite her," Chelsea said softly.

Tears welled up in Hannah's eyes. How could anyone be so nice to her when she was being so bad to Ginny?

"We won't even vote on it," Kathy said, smiling at Hannah.

Chelsea jumped up. "We have to finish here. I have to pick up a few groceries for Mrs. Witherspoon. She's too busy again this week to leave her house."

"What does she do?" Kathy asked as she opened the cupboard to get a can of furniture spray.

"She writes poetry, and she says when the muse . . . whatever that is . . . hits, she has to write. I guess it hit hard this time." Chelsea picked up the litter-box to empty it. "I was going to look *muse* up in the dictionary, but I forgot to."

Leaving the girls to work inside, Hannah ran to the garage for the lawn mower. The four of them traded jobs each day so they never had to get bored with any of them. This was her first time to mow the lawn. She wheeled the lawn mower out of the garage and onto the lawn, started it with a mighty roar, then walked behind it as it pulled her along. The sky was even grayer than before, but she didn't mind. She was glad the sun wasn't as hot as it had been yesterday. She walked faster as she thought about yesterday—about Ansell, Ginny, and even Lena.

The mower vibrated through her hands and almost to her elbows. The roar shut off any other sounds. But her brain whirled with thoughts of yesterday. She wished Ansell had never told her about his problem, or about Ginny's. She wished Lena could see how terrible Ginny was and stop copying her.

Suddenly Hannah stopped and the mower bucked, trying to keep going. Why wish for anything? Wishing didn't help! She let the mower pull her forward again, but instead of wishing, she prayed for Ansell and for Lena. Reluctantly she even prayed for Ginny—that she'd go home and that she'd stay away from Lena.

Finally Hannah finished the lawn and shut off the mower. What wonderful silence! She stood quietly, just enjoying the quietness. She wheeled the mower into the garage and shut the door with a rumble, then walked through the connecting door into the laundry room. She heard the girls talking and giggling in the kitchen and joined them. They sat around the table drinking cans of pop.

"I'm done." Hannah sank down in the only empty chair and opened the orange soda Chelsea handed her. She drank thankfully, letting the pop cool her mouth and run down her dry throat. The fizz tingled in her mouth and tickled her nose.

Chelsea spread her hands wide. "I have a fantastically great announcement."

"What?" the girls asked at once.

Hannah smiled at Chelsea's excitement.

"Mom said I can have all three of you sleep over at my house Sunday night. We can sleep in the basement and play all night if we want."

Hannah almost burst with happiness. She'd never slept over with anyone except family in her entire life. And to spend the night in Chelsea's fabulous basement that her dad had turned into a game heaven was too much. She was sure Mom would let her. "I can't wait!"

"What time do you want us?" Kathy asked.

"Seven. Or do you want to make it earlier?"

"It doesn't matter to me," Roxie said. "I'll be there."

Kathy pushed back her blonde curls. "I don't know. I'll ask my dad."

"What shall we bring?" Hannah asked.

Chelsea frowned thoughtfully. "We have enough blankets and pillows. Bring your pajamas, of course. And something good to snack on. No food is allowed that's good for us." She giggled. "I'm making chocolate-chip cookies with M & Ms. And apple juice. I love apple juice!"

"I know just what I'll bring!" Hannah could

barely sit still. "I learned how to make chocolate candy pieces full of nuts and coconut. It's soooo good!"

Roxie bounced on her chair, sending her cap of hair flying up. "I'll bring taco chips and bean dip. And a liter of Vernors."

"What's Vernors?" Chelsea asked.

"Like a ginger ale. Made here in Michigan. You'll like it."

"I'll stick with apple juice." Chelsea leaned toward Hannah. "What about Ginny? Shall we invite her?"

"No way!" Hannah shook her head hard. "No!"

Chelsea held up her hand. "Okay. Okay. We won't."

Hannah flushed. "Sorry."

Kathy jumped up. "I got to go right now. See you tomorrow . . . And Sunday night for sure!"

Just then thunder cracked, and they all jumped and shrieked.

"I guess we'd better all get going," Chelsea said, clearing off the table and grabbing the keys from the counter. "Kathy, don't worry about coming in the morning if it's raining. The three of us can take care of the work." Kathy was the only one of the Best Friends who didn't live right in The Ravines.

"Thanks." Kathy ran to the door.

Hannah watched out the window as Kathy jumped on her bike and rode away. "I hope she makes it home before it rains."

"I hope we all do," Roxie said as she headed for the door.

Hannah raced down the sidewalk and into her house just as a few giant raindrops hit the sidewalk. As she watched out the window the rain fell faster. The wind suddenly started to blow and lashed the rain against the windows. The trees swayed.

"Hannah, is that you?" Mom called from the living room.

"Yes."

"Did you see Ginny and Lena?"

A chill ran down Hannah's spine. "No." She ran to the living room where the twins were playing on the floor and Mom was rocking Burke. "Where'd they go?"

Mom frowned. "To find you."

"I was at the Crandalls'. Lena knows where that is."

Mom looked worried. "I wonder where they went."

"Lena knows to come home when it's raining out." Hannah nervously ran her hands up and down her arms. Would Lena come home if Ginny didn't want to?

"They said they were going to the Crandalls'," Mom said impatiently. "Where can they be?"

"If I knew, I'd go get them. But they could be anywhere!"

"I know." Mom sighed heavily. "If they aren't back when your dad gets home, he'll go look for them."

Hannah paced from one room to the other, looking out the windows often to see if she could see Lena or Ginny. Never in her life had Lena disobeyed the rule about running inside the minute bad weather came.

About an hour later the rain let up, and Hannah saw Lena and Ginny running toward the front door, acting as if nothing was wrong. Hannah flung the door wide.

"Where have you been? Mom's been worried," Hannah snapped as she jumped away from the raindrops falling off the girls.

"We're just fine," Ginny said, giggling.

"We had fun." Lena looked at Ginny and giggled as if she knew a secret.

Hannah tensed. Just where had they been? "Run in and tell Mom you're home and safe."

Lena ran to the living room, calling to Mom as she ran.

Ginny jabbed Hannah in the arm. "It won't do you any good to ask Lena where we've been. I swore her to secrecy. And I told her if she broke it I'd put a curse on her."

"How stupid!"

"She doesn't think so."

"Just leave her alone, Ginny! I don't want her hurt."

"Like you even care."

"I do care!"

Ginny shrugged, then giggled again. "We got ourselves a perfect place to hide out. Perfect. And you'll never find out where. Never!"

Hannah stalked to the kitchen, away from Ginny.

9

The Missing Money

Hannah paced her room while Dad talked to Lena in his study. Lena was in big trouble for not coming home when it started to rain. She was in even bigger trouble for not telling where she and Ginny had been for so long.

Hannah stopped at her window and looked out onto the backyard. The rain had stopped altogether, and the sun was shining again.

"Telephone, Hannah!" Mom called up the stairs.

Hannah ran to the hallway and picked up the extension. It was Kathy.

"Did you buy the Pampers yet for the Lawson baby?"

"No. I guess I forgot about it with the 4th and . . . you know." Hannah twisted the phone cord around her finger. "Shall I do it today?"

"Tomorrow's soon enough. The Lawson baby

is a girl. Buy the biggest pack you can with whatever money you have. I want to take them over tomorrow afternoon. Mom and some other ladies got baby clothes for her, so I'll take those too. Thanks, Hannah. See ya."

Frowning, Hannah started toward her room. How had she forgotten the good deed they'd decided to do for the Lawson family? She'd count the money now and maybe ride to the supermarket and get the Pampers yet tonight before it got dark out.

Just then Lena raced up the stairs, sobbing hard. She jabbed Hannah. "Daddy wants you right now. I hope he's as mean to you as he was to me!"

Hannah ran lightly downstairs and into Dad's study before something or someone else got his attention. He was standing at the French door looking out onto the deck. He turned and lifted a dark brow. He'd changed from his gray slacks and white shirt that he'd worn to work to a pair of jeans and a western shirt.

"Lena tells me you're having a hard time with Ginny," Dad said as he motioned for her to sit on the leather sofa.

She sank to the edge, the leather smooth against her hands. "Ginny's hard to get along with."

"I know. But I want you to try." He hoisted himself up on his desk and crossed his ankles. His dress shoes were off, and he wore black socks. He always wore cowboy boots with his jeans. His eyes softened with love as he looked at her. "What did you need to talk to me about that's so urgent?"

Hannah took a deep breath. "Ansell. Did you talk to him at the gathering yesterday?"

"No." Dad frowned thoughtfully. "What about him?"

She moved restlessly. "He needs help, Dad. Really bad!"

"Oh?"

In a rush of words she told him about talking with Ansell and all that he'd said. "First I promised I wouldn't tell anyone, then I said I would break my promise and tell you so you could help him. He was glad, Daddy! He was!"

Dad shook his head and looked concerned. "Ben never said a word. But he might not even know his son drinks."

"Will you help him?"

"Yes . . . If he'll let me."

"What about Ginny? Did Uncle Jonas send her here to get her away from drinking?"

Dad stood down from the desk and walked slowly to the sofa. He sat beside Hannah and took her hand. "Jonas said he sent her here to learn respect. He didn't say a word about drinking."

"Ansell said she does."

"Sometimes Ansell makes up stories to suit himself."

"He looked like he was telling the truth."

"Maybe. I'll find out."

Hannah sighed in relief. "What about Lena? What will you do about her?"

"What about her? I already spoke to her about disobeying."

Hannah looked down at the carpet, then up at Dad. "Lena does whatever Ginny says, even if it's wrong!"

"I talked to her about that. She won't do it again."

"Good!"

"I want you to be kinder to Ginny. Spend time with her. Maybe you could have her go with you to do a *King's Kids* job."

Hannah's heart sank. She could never do that!

"So, Hannah . . ."

She heard the laughter in his voice and looked at him questioningly. "What?"

"What are you buying me for my birthday? It's only two weeks away, you know."

She tried to smile. Every year he reminded all of them about his birthday, teasing them about what they'd buy. He always acted surprised when he got his gifts—like he thought they'd forget or something. Somehow she had to think of something really terrific for this year.

"Don't go overboard," Dad said, grinning impishly. "A new pickup would be nice. A red one.

Blue's my second choice. But I'll settle for a pair of boots or even a vacation to Scotland. I've always wanted to go to Scotland."

Hannah laughed. "I guess I'll have to return the airline tickets to Australia that I bought last week."

"Australia! Now there's a place to go." He laughed and hugged her tight. "I'll be glad for the trip."

She felt his heartbeat against her ear and smelled the slight odor of sweat. "I love you, Dad. Someday I will buy you and Mom a trip to Australia. And Scotland too!"

He kissed her cheek. "I love you, Wasson."

She flushed. *Wasson* meant "light all around." But because of her anger at Ginny, her light felt dim and dirty.

Dad jumped up. "I promised your mom we could go for a long walk. We'll take the twins and Lena and leave the baby home with you."

"Okay." Hannah slowly stood up. "What about . . . Ginny?"

Dad shrugged. "She can come with us or stay here."

Hannah wanted to yell, "Take her! Take her!" But she walked out of the study and into the living room. Mom had on her walking shoes, and the twins were impatiently waiting beside her. Burke was in his portable bed beside Mom's rocking chair.

"Burke's been fed and should sleep all the time

we're gone," Mom said. "Viv, run and get Lena, please. Tell Ginny she's welcome to go with us."

Vivian sped away, while Sherry did a somersault in front of the couch.

"Mom, Chelsea's having a sleepover at her house Sunday night and she invited me. The Best Friends will all be there." Hannah held her breath. "Will you let me go?"

Mom rubbed a hand across her wide forehead. "Are you sure she invited you?"

"Yes! I was surprised too. You can call her mom and ask if you want."

"No, I believe you. Sure, you can go."

Hannah hugged Mom tightly. "Thanks! Seven o'clock Sunday night."

"If Chelsea changes her mind, don't feel bad."

"She won't." Hannah's nerves tightened. But what if she did? Oh, she just couldn't!

A few minutes later everyone except Hannah and Burke left to go on a long walk. Hannah was thankful Ginny didn't stay home. Hannah laughed aloud as she bent down to the baby to make sure he was still asleep. He was. "It's just you and me, Burke." She twirled around the room and laughed.

She watched TV for a while, then remembered Kathy's phone call. She raced upstairs to count the money in the *King's Kids* money pouch. Her drawer stuck as she tried to open it. She jiggled it and finally it came open. She dug down in the corner and pulled out the pouch. It was empty!

"Ginny stole it! I know she did!" Hannah flung the empty bag back in the drawer and pushed it shut with a bang. "She's gone too far this time!"

Anger rushed through her as she looked around the bedroom. Maybe Ginny had hidden the money in her things. Hannah jerked open the drawer that she'd emptied for Ginny. Everything was crammed in it instead of neatly folded and stacked. Hannah searched the drawer, but didn't find any money. She looked in Ginny's purse that hung over the closet doorknob. She found a few dollars, but no pile of change. "She could've turned in the change for bills," Hannah muttered. She pulled out a five and some ones. Ginny had taken the *King's Kids* money, so she'd take it right back!

She stuffed the bills into the pocket of her jeans and ran downstairs to Burke. She'd have to wait until morning to buy the Pampers.

When the family returned, Hannah watched Ginny closely to see if she said or did anything to give away her guilt. But she didn't. She just kept going on and on about a white kitten she wanted.

"Hannah works at a place with white kittens," Mom said. "She'll take you there sometime and show them to you."

Ginny smiled at Hannah's mom, then turned

and frowned at Hannah. "Don't bother, Hannah. I know you don't want to."

"Of course she does," Dad said as he picked up baby Burke. "Don't you, Hannah?"

"We planned to carry them around the neighborhood to find homes for them," Hannah said weakly. "We'll bring them here."

"And we can see them too!" cried the twins, jumping up and down.

"I want one," Lena said, snuggling close to Mom. "Can I have one?"

"Sorry, Lena, but no." Mom nuzzled Lena's cheek and neck and laughed softly. "*You're* our sweet little kitten."

Lena giggled.

"Come on, Lena," Ginny said sharply. "Let's make plans for tomorrow."

Lena hugged Mom, then ran after Ginny.

"See, Dad?" Hannah said sharply. "Ginny calls, and Lena follows!"

Dad shook his head. "It's not that bad."

Hannah started to tell about the missing money, but the twins interrupted, and another good opportunity didn't come along.

The next morning Hannah rode her bike to the supermarket and bought a pack of Pampers for a baby girl, then rode fast to the Crandall house.

She found the girls in the kitchen and held the Pampers out to Kathy. "Here . . . I bought the size just up from Newborn since the baby is a month old."

"I'm glad you know about buying Pampers," Kathy said with a laugh. "Megan has been out of diapers for two years." The smile left her face. "She still plays with Natalie, her make-believe friend. Not like she did, but still, I thought she'd give her up by now."

They talked about their families for a while, checked the kittens, played with them, then went to work. They worked a short time each day at the Crandalls' so they never had to work really hard or really long. The Crandalls had said they'd be gone until September, but they wanted the house spotless at all times just in case they decided to cut their vacation short.

Back in the kitchen after they were finished, Chelsea opened the refrigerator and stuck her head in. "Who drank my apple juice? I left it yesterday so I'd have it today."

"I didn't," the girls all said at once.

"You probably finished it and forgot," Roxie said as she reached around Chelsea for a can of Sprite.

Hannah took a can of orange soda again and snapped it open. It was cold and delicious. She had bought a supply of pop and juice to keep in the refrigerator for them to drink at their break each day. It was fun to sit around the table and drink pop and talk.

"I have something terrible to report today," Hannah said, keeping her hands around the icy can.

"What?"

"About Ginny again, I bet," Kathy said.

"Can't you sleep over Sunday night after all?" asked Chelsea.

"I can sleep over."

"Yeah!" Roxie, Kathy and Chelsea shouted together.

"It's about the *King's Kids* money." Hannah took a deep breath and told the story. "So I just took money from Ginny's purse. I won't say anything until she does. She knows she's guilty, and when she sees the money is gone from her purse, she'll know I know. She won't say anything."

"I'd tell on her," Roxie snapped. "Maybe then your dad would send her home."

"He won't. He promised his brother he'd help her."

"That's nice of him," Kathy said. Then she sighed. "I know how hard it is to have your dad help someone. Brody is being such a jerk! I wish Dad would tell him to stay home where he belongs. But he won't. He just keeps spending time with him." Kathy made a face. "And now he says I have to too! I had to actually play a game with him last night!"

"Was it fun?" Roxie asked.

"That's not the point. But . . . yes, I had fun. It's just that I had no choice. That's not right!"

Just then the dogs barked, and the girls jumped, then giggled.

"I guess we'd better go," Chelsea said, cleaning off the table. "Tomorrow night, girls, is the sleepover! Oh, I can't wait!"

Hannah hugged herself while her heart leaped with excitement.

10

The Sleepover

Hannah laughed under her breath as she picked up her pack that held her newest pink pajamas, toothbrush and toothpaste, hairbrush, silver fingernail polish (in case anyone wanted to try it out), and the candy she'd made late last night. It was almost time to walk across the street to the first sleepover ever in her entire life. Shivers ran up and down her spine, and she couldn't move. During Sunday school and church, her mind kept drifting to the sleepover and to the possibility that Chelsea would change her mind. During dinner she'd waited for Chelsea to call and say she'd decided to have only Roxie and Kathy over. The phone had rung once, but it was for Mom about nursery duty at church next Sunday.

Just then Lena dashed into the bedroom, then stopped short when she saw Hannah. Lena had on blue shorts and T-shirt and a white towel wrapped around her head. Her black eyes looked huge in her small face. "I thought you were gone," she said in a tiny voice.

"I'm just going." Hannah started for the door, then stopped and looked at Lena. She looked very guilty. "What did you do?"

"Do?" How innocent she sounded!

"You and Ginny have been in the bathroom for ages." A shiver trickled down Hannah's back. "Did she cut your hair?"

"No! Don't be dumb!" Lena backed away, her hands holding the towel tightly to her head.

"Lena, what did she do?" Hannah eased her pack to the floor and stepped toward Lena.

"Don't touch me!" she cried.

"Lena!" Hannah grabbed the towel and tugged it hard. It fell away from Lena and landed on the floor at her feet. Spikes of strange-colored red hair stood out from her head. She looked ready to burst into tears. Hannah couldn't speak as she stared in horror at Lena. The silence went on and on and on.

"It's not bad when it's brushed out," Ginny said as she walked in."

Hannah spun around.

Ginny stopped short when she saw Hannah and gasped for breath. "You were supposed to be gone!"

Hannah clutched at her throat. Ginny's hair was the same awful red as Lena's! She'd brushed it neatly, but the color couldn't be brushed away. "What have you done?" croaked Hannah.

Ginny flung her hair back and tipped up her chin. "I wanted blonde hair. How was I to know it would turn red?"

"Yeah, how was she supposed to know?" asked Lena in a weak voice as she lightly touched her hair.

Hannah glared at Lena. "How could you let her do this to you?"

"I wanted blonde hair too."

Hannah shook her finger at Lena. "Wait'll Mom and Dad see you."

"Don't scare her!" snapped Ginny as she started to brush Lena's hair. "It's not as bad as it looks."

"Oh yes it is!"

Lena's eyes filled with tears.

"It'll grow out," Ginny said softly as she patted Lena's shoulder.

Hannah helplessly shook her head as she picked up her pack.

"Are you going to tell on me?" Lena asked tearfully.

"No. Your hair will tell on you." Hannah walked from the bedroom and down the stairs. She was going to a sleepover! Once again excitement bubbled inside her that not even Lena's terrible hair could dim.

"I'm going now," Hannah said as she walked into the kitchen.

"Have fun!" Mom answered.

Mom and Dad were popping corn. The delicious aroma floated all around Hannah.

She turned away, then turned back as she thought about telling on Lena.

"If you're nervous about going, just stay home," Dad said as he spooned melted butter over the bowl of fluffy white popcorn.

Mom slipped an arm around Hannah. "You go, Nanna. Don't let your nerves keep you home."

Dad crossed his arms over his thick chest and frowned. "Why does she even want to go?"

"They're her friends." Mom touched Hannah's cheek. "When I was your age no white girls asked me to sleep over. But times are changing. You have been invited, and you'll go. Maybe next week you can ask them all over here."

Hannah smiled. "I'd like that." But would they come?

Dad shook his head. "I don't know if baby Burke and me can stand even more girls around. It's a hard life, you know, being surrounded by females!"

"Don't listen to him, Hannah. He loves every minute of it."

"I know."

"See you tomorrow." Mom kissed Hannah's warm cheek. "You look pretty in your new clothes."

Hannah touched her plum-colored knit top and matching shorts. She'd taken forever to decide what to wear.

"Have fun," Mom said.

"I will." But would she?

Dad hugged her and kissed her. "If you have any candy left, bring it home for me."

She giggled. "I left some for you."

"Where? I already looked everywhere!"

"Look in the butter keeper in the refrigerator." Hannah giggled as Dad quickly opened the refrigerator and pulled out the small plastic bag of candy. It had taken her a long time to decide where to hide it so he wouldn't find it on his own.

"Thank you!" Dad kissed her again. "Do I have to share it with your mother?"

"Of course!"

"You'd better." Laughing, Mom reached for the candy, but Dad held it up high.

"See you tomorrow," Hannah said with a laugh as she walked out.

The sun was still bright and hot as Hannah ran across the street to Chelsea's. Was she too early or too late? Would she even know how to act at a sleepover?

She knocked on the back door, and Chelsea

immediately flung it open. She wore yellow shorts and a knit yellow and green top.

"Come in! Roxie's here, but Kathy's not." Chelsea looked ready to burst with happiness. "This is going to be sooo much fun!"

"I know," Hannah whispered. Was this a dream or was it really happening?

"We can stay awake all night if we want!" Roxie twirled around and laughed. She wore beige shorts with big pockets and a lime-green T-shirt.

"Mom says she doesn't care how late we stay up as long as we don't make so much noise that we keep them awake." Chelsea tapped Hannah's pack. "Set it by the basement door and we'll take it down when Kathy gets here."

Hannah set the pack down and walked to the kitchen with Chelsea and Roxie. A small tray of cut-up raw vegetables sat on the counter. The kitchen smelled like raw cabbage.

"Mom says we can't eat just junk food, so of course I had to agree." Chelsea wrinkled her nose.

"I like vegetables," Hannah said.

"So do I." Roxie picked up a small piece of cauliflower and ate it. "That's enough of the healthy stuff. Lead me to the chocolate cookies and pop!"

"Anything new with Ginny?" Chelsea asked as they sat at the table to wait for Kathy.

Hannah burst out laughing. "You won't believe

what she did this time! And to Lena too! Poor Lena!"

"What was it?"

"Ginny decided she wanted blonde hair. So, of course, Lena did too. Ginny will do anything to look white!" Hannah flushed and looked quickly at Chelsea and Roxie to see if they took offense.

"And I'd do anything to have your color instead of freckles all over me!" Chelsea touched her freckled arm, then Hannah's smooth brown one.

"So what happened?" Roxie asked.

"Their hair turned out a terrible red! A fake-looking red!"

The girls burst out laughing, and Hannah joined in. It *was* funny.

"Let's find an excuse to go over to your house after Kathy gets here so we can see them," Roxie said.

"We should!" Chelsea nodded and laughed harder, then sobered. "But I guess that would be too cruel."

Just then Kathy came, and Hannah had to tell the story all over again. Again they laughed until tears filled their eyes. Finally they loaded up all their stuff and walked to the basement.

Hannah had been to the special rec room to play or watch a video before, but it came as a delightful thrill each time she saw it. There was a pool table, a Ping-Pong table, a game table with a shelf behind it loaded with board games, a dart board on the wall, and a big-screen TV with Nintendo and a VCR. There were two couches that opened into queen-size beds and large multicolored throw pillows on the floor to sit on.

Chelsea opened a trifold door, and behind it was a snack bar with a refrigerator. She loaded the refrigerator with the food they'd all brought, unless it didn't need to be refrigerated, and set the rest of the things on the high counter.

Hannah pulled her special candy from her pack and set it on the counter. She'd put the candy in a plastic bowl that looked like it was made of glass and covered it with film. She sat on a high oak stool with a short back beside Kathy and pulled off the film. "Anybody want a piece of candy now?"

"I'll say!" Roxie snagged the first piece. She took a bite and said, "Mmmmmm . . . Good!"

Hannah smiled in delight. Last night while she made the candy she'd almost talked herself out of taking it just in case they all hated it. She took a piece and ate it. It was good!

They ate candy and talked, then had to have something cold to drink. They drank and talked and giggled. They walked to the huge pillows and sat down and talked some more.

Chelsea took a deep breath and said, "I looked at the calendar in the kitchen. You know, exactly two months from today school starts."

Hannah's heart sank. School! Maybe that would be the end of the Best Friends!

"At least we'll all be sixth graders instead of lowly fifth graders," Roxie said. "I am going to be in Photography Club and maybe try out for the Drama Club."

"I've made a terrible decision," Chelsea said.

"What?"

"You're going to bleach your hair!" Kathy exclaimed.

They all fell over giggling.

Chelsea took a deep breath. "Actually I am going to join the Computer Club and learn all I can about computers."

"No way!" Kathy cried, shaking her head. She brushed a cookie crumb off her bright orange T-shirt. "You hate computers."

"Rob said that as my big brother it's his place to convince me to learn computers since they are in our society to stay and if you don't know how to use them you're nowhere."

Hannah's heart sank lower and lower. When would the Best Friends have time for each other if they became involved in different activities?

Chelsea turned to Hannah. "You haven't said a word about what you plan to do. Drama? Music? Computers? What?"

"I haven't thought about it," Hannah said weakly. She had taken a computer class last year, but hadn't joined the club. She'd already learned that she wasn't accepted in any group as easily as white kids were.

"Art?" Kathy asked. "*I* might."

"I do like to paint with acrylics, but I'm not that good."

"I'm going to join the girls' softball team," Kathy said. "How about joining that, Hannah? You're good in sports."

"I'll think about it." Hannah looked down at the carpet. She had tried out last year, but hadn't made it even though a white girl who did worse than she did was put on the team.

"What about *King's Kids* during the school year?" Kathy asked.

Chelsea shrugged. "I guess we'll keep on with it. I can't get my phone bill paid before then, I don't think. But maybe we should work only on Saturday mornings."

"We could work a couple of hours after school if we had to," Roxie said. "We could see what our schedules are and go from there."

"I'd like to keep working," Hannah said.

"That's what we'll do." Chelsea tucked her long red hair behind her ears and trembled. "I hate starting school!"

"Why?" Kathy asked in surprise.

"New school . . . New teachers . . . New kids!

They'll make fun of my Oklahoma accent—and my freckles too. I just know it!"

Hannah knew something too. "We'll be there to help you."

"I wish we could all get in the same classes," Roxie said. "But there are three sixth-grade groups."

"I don't know what I'll do if none of you are in my classes!" Chelsea said with a shiver.

"Hey, this is a party! No more depressing talk about school." Roxie jumped up. "Who's ready to play a game or watch a video?"

Kathy ran to the shelf of board games. "I'm ready for a game! How about Clue? Or Aggravation?"

"Aggravation," Roxie and Chelsea said in unison.

"Clue," Hannah said because she loved solving mysteries. Chelsea's mom had taught them both games the last time she was over.

Kathy pulled out both games. "We'll play Aggravation first and Clue second. After that let's have your mom come play darts with us, Chelsea."

"She'll love it. But nobody has been able to beat her yet."

Just then the basement door opened, and someone started coming downstairs.

"Both Rob and Mike are gone for the night,"

Chelsea said. "And Mom and Dad are watching TV."

Hannah felt a funny tingle go over her, and when Ginny stepped into sight she knew why. She groaned loudly.

"Hello, everybody," Ginny said brightly. Her awful red hair hung over her shoulders and down her back. She wore Hannah's white shorts and lilac blouse. "I came to play some games with you."

Her heart sinking, Hannah looked helplessly at Chelsea.

11

Ginny

"Does Mom know you came here?" Hannah asked sharply.

Ginny shrugged. "Sure. They were busy beating up poor Lena."

"Because of her hair?" Roxie asked eagerly, then giggled.

"They wouldn't beat her," Hannah snapped.

"Did I say beat?" Ginny tossed her hair back. "They sure made her cry. And they took her to Uncle's study."

"Does my mom know you're here?" Chelsea asked.

"Sure. She said to go on down." Ginny looked at the games sitting on the table. "Aggravation! Hey, I'm good at that!"

The Best Friends looked at each other and struggled not to burst into a wild fit of giggles over

Ginny's hair and over the way she pushed her way in. That was aggravation for sure!

"Five can play it," Kathy said as she found a folding chair and set it at the table.

"I get the red marbles," Roxie said, dropping to a chair.

"Blue!" Ginny sat down and reached for the blue marbles.

Hannah flushed with embarrassment as she reached for the yellow marbles. Couldn't Ginny see how obnoxious she was?

Chelsea took the green and Kathy the black.

Roxie picked up the dice and handed each girl one die. "Roll to see who goes first. First six goes first, or highest goes first."

Ginny won the roll and started the game.

Soon they were so involved with the game that Hannah even forgot to be upset with Ginny. Chelsea won the first game, Ginny the second and Roxie the third.

"Now for Clue," Kathy said as she put away Aggravation and spread out Clue.

Ginny looked around the room, then jumped up and looked at everything. "This is really great! You're sure lucky, Chelsea."

"Thanks. I hated it when we first moved here, but I like it now." Chelsea told Ginny about living in Oklahoma, then moving to Middle Lake when her dad got a promotion and started working in Grand Rapids.

"We live near Lansing, and I hate it! I don't have any friends." Ginny suddenly stopped talking and looked away.

Hannah felt just a twinge of pity for Ginny. It vanished when she looked at Ginny's terrible hair and thought of poor Lena.

"Let's play Clue!" Kathy cried, waving the small black envelope. "I already put the killer, the room, and the weapon in place."

Ginny slowly sat back in her chair. "I'm not too good at Clue."

"Neither am I," Roxie said. "So don't feel bad."

"Hannah will win anyway," Chelsea said, tapping Hannah's arm. "She's great at figuring things out."

Hannah grinned.

"No way," Ginny said. "*I'll* win!"

Struggling to keep her temper, Hannah looked at her cards instead of at Ginny.

"Know what would be fun?" Ginny asked with a low laugh. "Going to an empty house and playing hide 'n seek and even sleeping there."

"We could tell ghost stories," Roxie said excitedly.

"At the Crandalls' house!" Ginny cried. "Lena

showed it to me. It would be perfect! Why not go there later and even spend the night?"

"Let's do it!" Roxie clapped her hands, and her eyes sparkled.

Hannah locked her hands in her lap and bit back the angry remark she wanted to fling at Ginny.

"We can't *play* in the Crandalls' house," Chelsea said in horror. "We have to take care of it and keep it nice."

Roxie sighed in disappointment. "I guess you're right, but it sure would be fun."

"I say we do it anyway," Ginny said. "The Crandalls won't know. And none of us would tell them."

"We're playing Clue right now," Kathy said. "Let's finish the game. I have a feeling I'll win."

Hannah felt the tension in the air as they started to play. Soon they got into the game, and the tension vanished. For a while it looked like Ginny was going to win, but Hannah did. They played a second game, and Kathy won.

"Let's get the chips and dip." Chelsea ran to the refrigerator and pulled out the dip and the vegetables.

Roxie tore open a fresh bag of chips, and everyone grabbed a handful.

"Is your brother Rob here, Chelsea?" Ginny asked with her mouth full.

"No. He and Mike are spending the night with

Nick and Gavin Rand." Chelsea propped her chin in her hands. "I liked Nick for a while, but he barely talks to me anymore."

"What does he look like?" asked Ginny eagerly.

Hannah rolled her eyes as Chelsea described Nick in great detail. They talked about boys a long time, while Hannah sat quietly and listened. Last year she'd liked Tom Nelson, but she stopped when he made fun of her last name by calling her Hannah Wigwam.

"Why don't we have a girl/boy party?" Ginny asked excitedly. "We could have it at the Crandalls'!"

"We can't," Hannah snapped.

"Forget about doing anything at the Crandalls'," Chelsea said kindly but firmly. "We work there, and we don't have permission for anything else."

"If you say so," Ginny said with a mischievous smile. "Then let's have a girl/boy party here." She waved her arm wide. "This is a perfect place for a party!"

"I'll talk to my mom." Chelsea didn't sound very excited about the idea.

"Time for another game," Kathy said as she ran to the shelf of games.

"No!" cried the others.

"I brought silver fingernail polish," Hannah said.

"Paint my nails!" Chelsea held her fingers out toward Hannah. "I brought some of Mom's makeup for us to use too."

Soon they were trying out eye shadow, blush, lipstick, and Hannah's nail polish. Ginny put Chelsea's hair in a french braid that looked beautiful on her, then moussed Kathy's curls back above her ears and spiked them on top of her head.

"I love it!" Kathy cried as she looked in the big, round hand mirror Chelsea had brought down.

"Do mine," Roxie begged.

Ginny parted Roxie's short dark hair on the side, moussed back one side, and draped the other side down almost over her eye.

Roxie stared at herself in the mirror. "With this makeup and hairstyle I could pass for a fifteen-year-old! It's sooo perfect!"

Jealousy rose inside Hannah. She turned away from the others and pretended to be reading a magazine Roxie had brought so they couldn't see how she felt. Why hadn't Ginny stayed away? Nobody had wanted her. Now suddenly it was like she was a friend.

"Are you spending the night, Ginny?" Roxie asked.

"No. Auntie said I must be back by 11."

Hannah breathed a sigh of relief while the others said how sorry they were. Couldn't they see how terrible Ginny was? Had they forgotten how she'd ruined Hannah's special dress on the 4th of July? It was at the cleaners without any promise they could get out the stain.

At 11 Ginny started toward the stairs. "I had fun," she said, and she sounded like she meant it.

"We'll walk you home." Chelsea jumped up and followed Ginny.

Hannah reluctantly walked upstairs with the others.

"I'll unlock the door so we can get back in without bothering Mom and Dad," Chelsea said, clicking the lock on the back door.

Outdoors, the street lights cast long shadows in the yards and over the street. The air was pleasantly cool. A dog barked a few houses away, and a truck rumbled past on the street outside the subdivision.

"Let's go to the park!" Ginny cried with her hands clasped at her heart.

"No!" snapped Hannah. Didn't Ginny ever follow the rules?

"We can't," Kathy said gently. "None of us are allowed to leave home after dark without an adult."

"I'll say I'm an adult."

"You're twelve!" Hannah knotted her fists.

"Well, I want to go to the park!" Ginny flipped her hair and raced off down the sidewalk.

"Come back!" Chelsea whispered as loudly as she could.

"Oh, that girl!" Hannah watched Ginny disappear in the darkness. She wanted to scream for her to come back, but she was afraid the whole neighborhood would hear her. "I'd better go after her."

"Wait!" Roxie caught Hannah's arm. "Tell your dad. He'll go get her."

"We'll come with you," Kathy said, and Chelsea agreed.

Hannah ran across the street to her house. The door was locked, so she rang the doorbell, then waited, standing on first one foot, then the other.

Finally Dad opened the door. He looked as if he'd been sleeping. He stared at the girls in surprise. "Hannah! Girls! What's wrong?"

"Ginny decided she wanted to go to the park. We tried to stop her."

"We did!" Chelsea agreed.

"She's upstairs asleep."

"No, Dad. She's been at Chelsea's the past three hours."

Hannah's dad shook his head and looked very grim. "Go on back to your sleepover. I'll take care of Ginny."

"Thanks, Dad."

"Thanks, Mr. Shigwam."

Silently the girls walked back to Chelsea's house and went quietly downstairs.

"I think we should pray for her," Kathy said quietly.

Chelsea nodded.

Hannah wanted to say, "I hate her! She doesn't deserve to have us pray for her!" But she nodded agreement with the idea.

"She's nice when she wants to be," Roxie said, touching her hair hanging down over the left side of her forehead.

The girls stood in the middle of the basement and held hands while Chelsea prayed. "Heavenly Father, take care of Ginny tonight so she doesn't get hurt or get in trouble. Let her know You love her. Help us to tell her about Jesus. In Jesus' name, Amen."

Hannah dropped Chelsea's and Roxie's hands and walked slowly to the snack bar. Ginny had ruined her sleepover!

"I'm ready for more pop and chips!" Roxie opened the refrigerator and pulled out the pop. "Anyone else?"

"Apple juice for me."

"I'll take Vernors."

"What about you, Hannah?"

"It doesn't matter."

Chelsea squeezed Hannah's hand. "We don't blame you for what Ginny did tonight. It was fun having her here, but I'm glad she left so we can get back to more fun."

Hannah lifted her head. "You mean we're not finished for the night?"

"No way! We still have a video to watch and stories to tell."

Hannah smiled as she reached for a can of orange soda.

"Do you suppose your dad found her?" Kathy asked.

"Probably. He'd come tell us if he didn't."

"Your dad is sure nice." Roxie ran her finger around the edge of her glass. "I was scared of him for a long time."

"Because he's Ottawa?" Hannah whispered, her stomach tight.

Roxie barely nodded.

Chelsea said, "A Cherokee man I met back in Oklahoma got drunk one night and killed five people."

"My dad doesn't drink."

"I know another Cherokee man back in Oklahoma who started a home for street kids. He got an award from the state for his good work. My dad went one Saturday of every month to play basketball or baseball with the boys. He said he wished he was able to do the good Tale Sweetwater was doing."

"My dad is always helping people. That's why Ginny's at our house now."

"I'd hate to have a dad who never helps anybody," Roxie said. "I used to be ashamed of my dad just because of the way he dresses sometimes and the way he acts sometimes. But I was wrong. I love my dad."

"Me too," Chelsea said. "I thought I hated mine for making us move here. But I wouldn't have three best friends if I lived back home."

"I wouldn't have any best friends," Hannah whispered.

Roxie squirmed on the bar seat. "Once when I was little I saw a black family at the supermarket. I guess I'd never noticed black people before that. But I saw them, and I got really scared . . . I don't know why. I never told anybody that before."

Kathy pushed her glass away and folded her hands on the counter. "Last year I saw a street person—a woman who lived out of a shopping cart. She was dirty and really really ugly. I was so scared I ran to the other side of the street so I wouldn't have to be near her. I never told anybody that before either."

"I hate it when I get scared," Chelsea said. "My mom says we get scared of people and things we don't understand. I wonder what Ginny's scared of."

Hannah frowned. "What makes you think she's afraid of anything?"

"I really don't know . . . But she acts like it sometimes."

"Maybe we could find out," Kathy said.

"I don't think I want to," Hannah whispered hoarsely. "I just want her to go home where she belongs. I don't want Dad to help her, and I don't want her hanging around here making trouble wherever she goes."

"Maybe she's afraid nobody will ever like her." Roxie brushed at her hair with her hand. "I was like that for a long time."

"Maybe if she acted right, people *would* like her." Hannah ducked her head. She knew that wasn't really true. She usually acted right, but not everyone liked her.

They sat quietly a long time, and then Chelsea jumped off her stool. "It's time to watch the video! I got this really great movie you'll love!"

"I'll grab the chips!" Roxie shouted.

"I'll get the cushions" Kathy volunteered.

Hannah helped Kathy with the cushions. They dropped them in a row far enough back from the big-screen TV so they could see the picture clearly. Chelsea popped in the video, and the music rolled out with the credits.

Hannah sank down on her stomach and rested her arms on the fat cushion. She wouldn't think about Ginny any more tonight. She'd watch the video and do whatever else they'd planned for the rest of the sleepover. She yawned, then stifled it. She would not go to sleep! This was a sleepover, and she wanted to be awake for it all.

12

A Mystery

The next day, back in her own house, Hannah jerked awake in time to see Ginny angrily slam a pillow down toward her. She rolled away, and the pillow just missed her. Her heart raced as she stared at Ginny. "What are you doing?" she cried as she jumped to the corner of her bed to get away from Ginny.

"How dare you send Uncle after me last night!" Ginny flung the pillow at Hannah. "I hate you!"

Hannah caught the pillow and tossed it over onto Lena's bed where it belonged, then climbed off the bed. She'd come home about 11 that morning after agreeing to meet the Best Friends at the Crandalls' at 3, ate a quick sandwich, then had flopped into bed to catch up on the sleep she'd missed last night. It was now two o'clock. She glared at Ginny. "I sure couldn't let you go to the park alone. Do you know what could've happened to you?"

"So what? Who cares anyway?" Ginny knotted her fists and paced the room in quick, angry steps. "I hate it here! I want to go home!"

"Then go! What's keeping you here?"

Her chest rising and falling, Ginny glared at Hannah. "My dad forced me to come. I can't leave."

"Why are you here?" Hannah stood very still. Maybe now she'd learn the truth.

Ginny opened her mouth, snapped it closed, and tossed her head. "You'd love to know and gloat, wouldn't you? Miss Perfect Odawa! Miss Perfect Daughter! I get sooo tired of hearing about you!"

Hannah sank to the edge of her bed and stared in shock at Ginny. "What are you ranting about?"

Ginny threw up her hands, then let them fall at her sides. "What's the use? You hate me as much as everybody else does. Even Auntie does now because I sneaked over to Chelsea's house last night. And she grounded me. Grounded! I've never been grounded in my life!"

"Then how do your folks punish you when you disobey or do something else wrong?"

Ginny frowned. "They don't." She sank to the edge of Lena's bed. She picked up Lena's pillow and hugged it. "They send me off to a relative."

"Is that why you're here?"

"Wouldn't you like to know?"

"What's the use in talking to you. You don't want help from my folks or from me." Hannah got out of bed, jerked her bedcovers into place, then pulled on clean green shorts and a white T-shirt. She pinned her *I'm A Best Friend* button in place. "I'm going downstairs to talk to Mom."

"She took the kids and went somewhere."

"Why didn't you go?"

"I'm grounded, remember?"

"What about Lena?"

"Oh, she went with them. They're really mad at me because of her hair. How was I to know it would turn red?" Ginny touched her terrible red hair and frowned. "And how was I to know she'd try to cut it all off?"

Hannah gasped. "Lena cut her hair?"

Ginny nodded grimly. "It was awful! And so uneven. Auntie cried, but the twins giggled."

"When will they all be back?"

"I don't know . . . And I don't care."

"I have to leave before 3."

"I just might sneak off to the mall and go shopping. I saw a skirt I'd like."

"Won't you ever learn?" Hannah brushed her hair in long, quick strokes. "You're grounded. That means you can't leave the house."

"Who's here to know the difference?"

"*You'll* know." Hannah pulled her hair back

and wrapped a wide green band around it. "And I'll know—and Jesus too."

"Tattletale!" Ginny flounced to the closet and grabbed her purse off the closet door. "I'll be back before they are." She stormed out, slamming the bedroom door hard enough to make a picture on the wall almost fall off its nail.

Hannah sighed and shook her head. "I wonder why she is here?" Hannah muttered as she slowly walked out to the hall and down the stairs. The house was unusually quiet. The only smell was a hint of fabric softener from the laundry room.

Hannah's stomach growled with hunger, surprising her after the ton of junk food she'd eaten last night. In the kitchen she pulled a cookie from the cookie jar, made a face, and put it back. She got an apple from the refrigerator and ate it as she walked toward the Crandalls'. The juice sprayed on her face, and she wiped it off with her hand.

Piano music drifted out from Ezra Menski's house, and Hannah stopped on the sidewalk in surprise. While she stood there Roxie ran up.

"What's wrong, Hannah?"

"Piano music. Isn't that strange?"

Roxie's face turned bright red. "It's my grandma!" Roxie ran up the steps of Ezra's house and rang the doorbell. She turned and frantically motioned for Hannah to join her.

Reluctantly Hannah ran to Roxie's side. "What's wrong, Roxie?"

"Grandma's playing the piano for Ezra. I don't want her hanging out with him!" Roxie punched the doorbell again. From inside Gracie barked.

"But why not?"

"I just don't! He's mean. Besides, how would Grandpa feel?"

"Roxie, your grandpa is in Heaven."

"I know! But he still wouldn't want Grandma hanging around Ezra Menski of all people."

The door burst open, and Ezra stood there with a scowl on his face. "Why are you ringing the bell like it's the end of the world or something?"

"I want to see my grandma." Roxie tried to push past Ezra, but he blocked her way. She peered around him and shouted, "Grandma! It's me . . . Roxann."

Hannah hung back, flushing with embarrassment. Why was Roxie being so rude?

Emma Potter eased around Ezra and looked at Roxie questioningly. "Is something wrong, Roxann?"

"Why are you here?" Roxie snapped.

"To visit Ezra, of course." Emma Potter nodded and smiled at Hannah, then turned back to Roxie. "Do you want to join us? I'm playing the piano for him. After that we're going to take a walk to the park."

"She's not welcome in my house if she's going to act like a brat," growled Ezra.

Roxie jumped back. "I'm not acting like a brat!"

Emma Potter hugged Roxie. "Of course you're not. You're overly concerned about me, that's all. But I'm just fine. I've been on my own a lot of years, and I can take care of myself. Thank you for caring." She smiled as she ran a finger down Roxie's cheek. "Now, do you want to join us?"

"No," Roxie whispered. "I'm going to work with Hannah. I was just surprised you were here." She looked up at Ezra. "I'm sorry for being rude."

"I forgive you." He smiled, totally changing his gruff look to a pleasant one.

Roxie grabbed Hannah's arm, and they walked away together. "I am so embarrassed!" Roxie whispered. "I can't believe what I just did."

Hannah smiled at Roxie. "You were trying to protect your grandma. But you don't have to worry." She walked around a toy truck in the middle of the sidewalk. "Ezra really is a nice man. He just sounds and looks mean."

"I don't want Grandma to fall in love with some other man." Roxie brushed at her eyes with the back of her hand. "I heard on TV about this mean man who married old women for their money."

"Ezra and your grandma are the same age, and he wouldn't marry her for her money."

Roxie kicked at a stone on the sidewalk and sent it flying onto the grass. "I don't want him marrying her at all!"

"They might not even be thinking of that. They could just be friends."

"I guess." But she didn't sound very sure.

"You won't believe what Ginny did," Hannah said to get Roxie's mind off her grandma.

"What?"

Hannah stopped at the Crandalls' back door. "She sneaked out of the house last night to go to the sleepover. Now she's grounded, but she ran off to the mall to go shopping."

Roxie shook her head. "I can't believe that girl! What'll she do next?"

Hannah shrugged as they walked inside. "Roxie and I are here!"

"In the kitchen!" Chelsea called.

They hurried to the kitchen, where Chelsea and Kathy sat at the table. They both looked tired.

"Wait'll you hear what I did," Chelsea said almost in tears.

Hannah sank to the chair beside her, while Roxie sat across from her. "What?" they asked together.

Chelsea shook her head, her face as red as her

hair. "I know I shouldn't have, but I bought those jeans I told you about."

"Oh, Chelsea," Hannah said sadly. "Your phone bill!"

"I know, I know."

"Can you return them?" Roxie asked.

"I guess. But I won't do it! I want those jeans so bad!"

"You told me you absolutely must obey your parents," Roxie said. "The Bible says so."

Chelsea hung her head. "I know."

"We'll help you return them," Kathy offered.

"You don't know how cute they are!"

Hannah touched Chelsea's arm. "We promised to help each other."

"They look sooo good on me!"

"We wouldn't be true friends if we let you disobey."

Chelsea jumped up, her fists clenched at her sides. "I knew I shouldn't say anything! I knew I should just wear them and enjoy them. But I wanted all of you to be happy for me and to tell me how good they look on me."

Kathy shook her head. "You already knew how we'd feel, Chel. You told us so we could help you do the right thing."

"You know you did," Hannah said gently.

Chelsea burst into tears and covered her face

with her hands. "I know you're right," she agreed, sobbing. "But they're so cute. I want them so bad!"

"Not bad enough to disobey to get them." Roxie stood up and put her hands on her hips. "You are going to return those jeans, and we are going to help you. And that's that!"

Chelsea giggled between sobs. Finally she dried her eyes, blew her nose, and said, "We'll take them back when we're finished here."

"Good!" the others chorused.

"Now we'd better get to work." Chelsea sounded all business again. "It won't take us long since we don't have to mow the lawn or weed the flower beds." She quickly assigned them rooms. "We'll meet back here when we're done and then work together in here."

Hannah quickly opened the windows in the bedrooms to air them, dusted, then vacuumed the minute Kathy finished with the vacuum cleaner. She closed the windows, then frowned as she stopped inside the last bedroom. Who had pulled the bedspread off to the side that way? She quickly pulled it in place, fluffed the throw pillows, and stacked them near the head of the bed where they should've been.

Shrugging, Hannah ran to the kitchen. She was the first one there. Her mouth was dry, and she wanted a drink of water. Orange pop didn't sound good at all after last night. She opened the cupboard and pulled out a glass. She reached to turn on the faucet, then stared in horror at a broken glass in the sink. Who had broken it? Gingerly she lifted the pieces out of the sink and set them on the counter. She filled her glass and drank, then washed it out, rinsed it, and set it in the drainer.

The girls hurried in, and Roxie immediately opened the refrigerator.

"Hannah!" Chelsea cried. "You broke a glass!"

Hannah's heart sank. "No! I found it in the sink. I thought one of you did it."

"Not me," they all said at once.

"But somebody had to do it." Hannah looked at the others. "Could it happen and we not know it?"

"Like an accident?" Roxie asked, looking right at Hannah.

Hannah trembled. Roxie didn't believe her! Would they want to blame her because she was Native American? She moistened her dry lips with the tip of her tongue. "It was in the sink already broken," she whispered. "Honest."

"I believe you," Chelsea said with a smile. She turned to Roxie and Kathy. "She does not lie!"

Kathy smiled and nodded.

Roxie frowned. "Then who did do it? It couldn't jump in the sink itself."

"Here's a real mystery for you to solve,

Hannah." Chelsea tapped Hannah's shoulder. "It should be as easy as winning a game of Clue."

"Who else has access to the house?" Hannah leaned against the counter as her brain whirled with answers to the puzzle.

"No one," Kathy said.

"The dogs and cats," Roxie suggested.

"Yes!" Hannah nodded. "A glass could've been sitting on the counter beside the sink, and one of the animals could've knocked it into the sink, breaking it."

"That's possible," Kathy said.

Chelsea tapped her lips with her finger and narrowed her eyes. "But I cleaned in here Saturday. And I didn't leave a glass on the counter."

Suddenly Ginny ran into the kitchen, her eyes blazing. She shook her finger at Hannah. "You stole my money right out of my purse, didn't you?"

Hannah gasped and helplessly shook her head. "I would never do that!"

"Then where did my money go? I brought the blouse I wanted up to the check-out, went to pull out my money, and it was gone! You took it!"

Hannah shook her head hard, making her ponytail swish across her back. Then she remembered taking the money from Ginny. But it was *King's Kids* money, not Ginny's.

"Just look how guilty she looks!" Ginny cried.

Hannah felt hot all over. "I am not guilty!"

"Then why do you look like it?" Roxie asked sharply.

Hannah turned to Roxie and cried, "I knew you didn't really like me! Best friends believe each other!"

"Best friends tell each other the truth," Roxie snapped.

With a strangled cry Hannah ran from the kitchen and out the back door. The truth was finally out. She was Ottawa Indian, and Roxie would never accept her as a best friend. Roxie might even convince the others to kick her out of *King's Kids*.

13

Best Friends

Hannah sobbed harder and harder as she ran away from the Crandall house toward home. The hot sun burned down on her, making her hair damp with sweat. She almost tripped outside Ezra Menski's house, but caught herself and sped on. This was probably the end of her being part of the Best Friends. They'd tear up her signed Best Friends Pact and never speak to her again unless they were forced to. She didn't have to wait for school for them to drop her—they already had.

Just then Kathy whizzed around Hannah and stopped her bike right in Hannah's way. "Stop! We want to talk to you!"

"No!" Hannah dodged around the bike and ran across the street toward her house. She fished in the pocket of her green shorts for her key. If she could get inside, she'd lock them all out, then cry until her eyes fell right out of her head.

At her front door she fumbled with her key, almost dropped it, and finally got the door unlocked.

Meanwhile, Kathy dropped her bike, ducked around Hannah, and held the door wide. Her blonde curls stood out all over her head. Her face was red and her eyes full of concern. "Hannah, we're going to talk."

"No!"

"You and I will wait right here for the others."

"Get out of my house."

"We're going to talk to you."

Hannah helplessly shook her head.

"You hear me, Hannah?"

She stared at Kathy, too shocked to move. She sounded more like Roxie than her usual gentle self.

Chelsea, Roxie, and Ginny pushed their way inside, and Chelsea closed the door.

"Now *you're* in trouble," Ginny said with a wicked laugh.

"She is not!" Chelsea snapped.

Her face red, Roxie shook her finger at Hannah. "You stop thinking I don't like you because you're Native American!"

"It's true," Hannah whispered brokenly, her chest rising and falling.

"I *do* like you! But you did look guilty."

"Because you are guilty! Aren't you?" Ginny pushed her face right into Hannah's. "Aren't you?"

Hannah fiercely brushed away her tears.

"Give her a chance to talk," Kathy said.

Her hands locked together, Hannah faced Ginny. "I took money from your purse."

The Best Friends gasped.

"I knew it," Ginny gloated.

"But it was *King's Kids* money, not yours."

"That's not true!"

Hannah turned to her friends and quickly reminded them about finding her money pouch empty and why she knew she could take the money back from Ginny. "So it was mine to take!"

Ginny shook her head hard. "No way! I didn't take the money from the money pouch. I knew it was in your drawer, but I didn't take it."

"Then who did?" Hannah snapped.

"Who has access to your drawer?" Chelsea asked.

"The whole family. But none of them would steal. Only Ginny would."

"But I didn't!"

"I think she's telling the truth," Kathy said. Roxie and Chelsea agreed.

"Who else would take it?" Kathy asked.

Hannah shook her head. "Nobody."

"What if your mom needed change?"

"She'd tell me she took it, and she'd pay me back."

Chelsea took a deep breath. "What about . . . Lena?"

Hannah pressed her hand to her racing heart. Lena! What if she'd taken the money? She had been doing other bad things. She might steal.

"She's mad enough at you to do it," Ginny said smugly.

"If she did, it's all your fault." A muscle jumped in Hannah's jaw. "You've been turning her into a disobedient brat."

Pain flashed across Ginny's eyes, then was gone so fast Hannah didn't know if she'd really seen it. Ginny spun on her heels and raced to the stairs and dashed on up. The door slammed, and then all was quiet.

Hannah stood quietly for a long time. Finally she found the courage to look at the girls. They didn't look angry. "I'm sorry," she whispered.

"Don't ever think we don't want you as a best friend," Roxie said. "We do!"

"We do!" Chelsea and Kathy agreed.

Hannah blinked away fresh tears. "Thank you. It's just that I've never had real friends before."

"Well, now you have us!" Chelsea squeezed Hannah's hand.

"And you have to put up with a big mouth like mine," Roxie said.

"And friends who run you down with a bike." Kathy wrinkled her nose and smiled.

"And friends who buy jeans when they aren't supposed to. Now it's time to help me return my jeans."

Hannah nodded. "Sure. What are friends for anyway?" She giggled, and the others joined in.

Later, after Hannah returned from the mall and the Best Friends went to their homes, she walked slowly into her house. She heard voices in the kitchen. Her nerves tightened. Had Ginny made up some huge story about her stealing her money?

Hannah peeked into the kitchen. Mom was making dinner. The twins sat at the table coloring, and Burke was in his little bed in the middle of the table.

Hannah walked softly to the living room. Ginny was watching TV. Where was Lena?

Her heart racing, Hannah ran lightly upstairs and into the bedroom. Lena sat in her bed with her stuffed bear held tightly in her arms. She looked different. Her hair was cut as short as Roxie's, and it was black again.

"Hi," Hannah said softly.

Lena looked at Hannah with big sad eyes.

Hannah had planned to yell at Lena until she learned the truth about the missing money, but she couldn't with Lena looking so sad. "I see your hair is black again."

"Mom took me to a salon and had it cut and dyed." Lena rubbed the back of her hand across her nose. "I'm going to stay in here forever where nobody can see me with short hair."

"You look cute."

"I look ugly. I *am* ugly!"

"No, you're not."

"Don't talk to me now, Hannah." Lena's voice broke. "Mom says she wants me to think about my actions. She says I have to decide if I am going to follow Jesus or Ginny."

"It's better to follow Jesus. He loves you. Ginny keeps getting you in trouble."

"I know." Lena pressed her face down against her bear.

With a long sigh Hannah slowly walked out of the bedroom so Lena could be alone. She stopped in the hallway with her head down and her heart heavy. What could she do to help Lena?

Hannah shrugged, and tears pricked her eyes. There was nothing she could do for Lena, so why bother to try?

14

Lena

From Mr. and Mrs. Guthrie's kitchen window Hannah watched them drive out of their driveway. Then she turned and looked at the three kids she'd be watching until 11. Chelsea had been assigned to the job, but the last minute couldn't go, so she'd called Hannah. She was relieved to get out of the house. She didn't want to see Lena's sad face or be on edge while she waited for Ginny to tell Mom and Dad Hannah had stolen her money right from Ginny's purse.

Hannah forced away thoughts of her family so she could take care of the three kids. Eight-year-old Bobby sat at the table bent over his watercoloring with Sara, six, watching him. Four-year-old Timmy, already wearing his pajamas, lay on the floor pushing a toy truck around. Since Hannah had watched them two other times, she knew them and the house.

"Bobby hates me," Sara said, her dark eyes wide and glistening with tears.

"Why do you say that?" Hannah asked as she slipped an arm around Sara.

"He won't ever let me use his paints."

"She messes them all up," Bobby said, looking up with a scowl. He had red paint on his cheek and a smudge of blue on the tip of his nose.

"I do not." Sara folded her arms on the table and rested her head on her arms. "I am very careful."

"You're not gonna use my paints or my paper." Bobby bent back over his work, carefully stroking orange across his paper.

Hannah tugged on Sara's hand. "Let's see where your Barbie doll is. We could dress her in her ballerina stuff."

"Do you really want to?"

"Sure." Hannah smiled at Sara, and she finally smiled back.

They played several minutes, then Hannah excused herself so she could check on Timmy. He had fallen asleep on the floor. Hannah carefully carried him to his bedroom, put him in bed, and kissed his round pink cheek. She turned and almost tripped over Sara.

"He's asleep," Hannah whispered.

"Barbie's asleep too. I'll tuck her into bed. Want to help?"

"Sure." Hannah followed Sara across the hall to her room.

Sara pulled her covers back and laid Barbie down, then carefully covered her up and kissed her. "Now shall we watch TV or get a snack?"

"Whatever you want."

"I want to do what you do."

"Let's get a snack. I like graham crackers," Hannah suggested.

"Me too!"

"I like to dip them in milk."

"Me too." Sara giggled as she slipped her hand into Hannah's.

In the kitchen Hannah set out the crackers and milk while Sara climbed up on the stool at the counter.

"We have fun together, don't we?" Sara smiled.

"Sure do." Hannah poured milk into cups for Sara and herself. She broke off a cracker and dipped it in the milk, then ate it. Sara did the same thing. Hannah wiped her mouth with a napkin. Sara copied her. Hannah broke a cracker in half. So did Sara.

Suddenly a picture of Lena with Ginny flashed across Hannah's mind. Lena copied Ginny because Ginny paid attention to her. Hannah nodded. It was just like Sara with her. If she gave Lena love and attention, would she want to copy her instead of Ginny?

At 9 Hannah tucked Sara into bed, kissed her good night, then walked to Bobby's room to tuck him in. His walls were covered with his paintings.

"These are beautiful, Bobby."

"Thanks." He sat in his bed and looked around the room. "I like to look at them."

"Do you think Sara would?"

"She doesn't like me or my paintings."

"Sure, she does. I wonder if she'd like one hung in her room."

Bobby jumped off his bed. "I think she'd like this one. It's her Barbie doll dancing a ballet."

Hannah studied the swirl of colors. They did look like a ballet dancer. She smiled. "I think she would like it."

"I'll give it to her!" Bobby ran to Sara's room.

Hannah followed and stood in the doorway as Bobby presented the painting to Sara, showing her in detail what the painting was.

"I love it, Bobby!" Sara said excitedly.

"I'll hang it on the bulletin board for now," Hannah said, taking the painting and carefully pinning the edges to the board. "Tomorrow your mom can help you hang it where you want it."

"It's beautiful!" Sara held up her Barbie. "See what Bobby gave me, Barbie? He does like me, I think."

Bobby grinned and ran back to his room.

Off and on for the rest of the time at the

Guthries' Hannah thought of Lena. Hannah finally decided she would spend more time with Lena. Maybe she'd even show her the paper Chelsea had given her on how to make friends.

Hannah leaned back in the big overstuffed chair in the living room and waited for the Guthries to come home. She closed her eyes and quietly prayed for Lena. She even prayed for Ginny.

Later Hannah sat in the car beside Mr. Guthrie. She could hardly stay awake. They drove past the Crandall house, and she shot straight up. There were lights on at the Crandalls'!

"Is something wrong?" Mr. Guthrie asked, slowing the car.

"I don't know. I guess not."

He dropped her off in the driveway. She told him thanks for the ride and ran to the door. The cool breeze ruffled her hair. She thought about running to the Crandall house to check on it, but slipped inside her house instead. Maybe the Crandalls had come home tonight. Should she call Chelsea and ask?

"Hi, honey." With Burke on her shoulder Mom walked toward Hannah. "How did it go?"

"Fine."

"Chelsea called and wants you to call her back no matter how late it is."

"Thanks." Her pulse fluttering, Hannah hurried to the kitchen to use the phone there. Chelsea answered on the first ring.

"I can't work at the Crandalls' in the morning, Hannah. Would you get the key, unlock the door, and assign the work please?"

"Of course." Hannah bit her lip. "I was just past the Crandalls' and there are lights on at their house."

"No!"

"Maybe they're home."

"They can't be. I just talked to Sonya Crandall an hour ago."

"Maybe we left the lights on." Hannah gripped the receiver.

"We didn't. I double-checked. I always double-check."

Hannah shivered. "Should we go look?"

"Dad's still awake. I'll ask him to go with me."

"I want to go too."

"Okay. Come right over."

"I'll tell Mom." Hannah hung up and ran to the living room, where Mom was nursing Burke. Hannah quickly told her what was happening. "I'll be back soon."

"Okay. I'll wait up for you."

Hannah smiled and ran out of the house and across the street. Chelsea and her dad were just walking out their door.

"We're off to a real adventure," Chelsea's dad said with a chuckle.

"This is serious, Dad."

"I know."

As they hurried down the sidewalk Hannah shivered even though it was warm out. Would Roxie think she'd left the lights on?

Outside the Crandalls' Hannah stood on one side of Glenn McCrea and Chelsea on the other side. The house looked empty, but every light was indeed on.

Chelsea fished the key from her pocket and handed it to her dad. "This is scary," she whispered.

"Somebody's playing tricks on you." Glenn McCrea unlocked the door and stepped inside. He stood quietly. Suddenly both dogs started barking and raced to the kitchen.

Chelsea quieted them.

Hannah looked around, trying to find a clue. Who had come into the house and turned on all the lights? She thought of the broken glass and the messed-up bed upstairs. Had the same person broken the glass and messed up the bed? She followed Mr. McCrea and Chelsea through the house, turning lights off as they went. Nothing seemed out of place. Back downstairs again she looked in the sink. Nothing was there. She looked in the refrigerator. The pop was gone! She looked in the cupboard where they put the empties until they could take them in for a refund. The box was full!

"Look!" Hannah cried, pointing.

146

"Somebody has been here!" Chelsea shook her head helplessly. "Dad?"

"Sure enough." Mr. McCrea looked in the trash and found several dirty paper plates, a potato chip bag, and an empty chip dip container. "Did you girls have a party?"

They stared at each other and shook their heads.

"Ginny wanted to have a party here, but we wouldn't let her," Hannah said.

"Maybe she had one anyway," Mr. McCrea said.

Hannah groaned.

"How would she get in?" Chelsea asked. "I have the only key."

"Let's check the windows and other doors."

Hannah followed Chelsea and her dad through the house again. All the windows were locked, and so were the doors. "This is a real mystery," Hannah said as Mr. McCrea locked the door again and handed Chelsea the key.

"I'll keep my eye on the place," Chelsea's dad said as they walked home.

"And I'll look for clues again tomorrow," Hannah told them.

"If they're there, you'll find them." Chelsea smiled.

Outside the McCreas' Hannah took the

Crandalls' house key from Chelsea and slipped it into her pocket.

"I'll talk to you the minute I get home tomorrow," Chelsea said. "Maybe you'll have the mystery solved by then."

"Maybe." Hannah said good night and ran across the street to her house. She reported what had happened to Mom, then hurried to bed. She yawned, almost too tired to brush her teeth.

Just as she slipped between the covers Ginny moaned in her sleep and flung her arm across Lena.

With a sharp cry Lena sat bolt upright.

"It's all right, Lena," Hannah whispered. "Ginny must be having a nightmare."

Lena crawled out of her bed and walked across to Hannah. "I had a terrible nightmare too."

Hannah was too tired to talk, but she remembered Sara Guthrie and her need for love and attention. Sara had responded to love, and Lena might too. "You'll be all right, Lena. Go back to bed. I'll leave the door open a bit so the hall light shines in here."

Lena moved from one foot to the other. "Could I . . . sleep with . . . you?"

"I thought you wanted to sleep with Ginny."

"I do." But Lena didn't move.

Hannah pulled the covers back more. "Get in."

Lena jumped in beside Hannah and pulled the cover to her chin. "It was a terrible nightmare. I had

148

it once before, and Ginny said I should hang a dream catcher over the bed."

"I thought Ginny hated being Ottawa and didn't believe in dream catchers."

"She said it might work."

"Lena, Jesus loves you. He'll give you a peaceful sleep."

Lena sighed. "I know. Will you pray for me?"

Hannah hesitated, then said, "Sure." She turned on her side and touched Lena's shoulder. "Heavenly Father, please give a peaceful sleep to Lena. Take away whatever's causing the bad dreams. Fill Lena with Your peace. In Jesus' name, Amen."

"Amen," Lena whispered. "I think I know what's causing the bad dreams."

"What?"

Lena gripped the cover. "I . . . I took the *King's Kids* money."

Hannah gasped. "But why?"

"I wanted to buy a special gift for Dad's birthday. I was mad at you and mad because I couldn't be a *King's Kid*."

"Did you already spend it?"

"No," Lena said in a tiny voice.

"Good. Tomorrow you can put it back." Hannah would give it to Ginny. She brushed Lena's hair back. "Maybe we can put our money together and buy Dad something."

"Thanks, Hannah." Lena smiled, turned on her side, and fell asleep.

Hannah smiled. It hadn't been hard at all to help Lena. She'd do it from now on no matter what. And she would help her learn how to make friends. "I promise, Lena," she whispered softly.

15

The Surprise

As she chewed her Cheerios, Hannah peeked at Ginny slowly eating her toast. They were the only ones at the kitchen table. Had Ginny found a way to sneak into the Crandall house? Was she the mystery intruder? She had talked about a sweet white kitten she'd played with. She had known right where the kitchen was when she'd burst in and accused Hannah of stealing the money.

"What?" Ginny asked sharply.

"What what?" Hannah asked with a slight frown.

"Ever since Uncle left for work you've been watching me. I don't like it."

"I've been thinking about your idea of having a party at the Crandalls'." Hannah wiped her mouth with a white paper napkin.

Ginny stiffened. "What about it?"

"You already had it, didn't you?"

"What are you talking about?"

"Don't deny it, Ginny Shigwam! It'll be easy enough to find out. I'll ask around the neighborhood to see who was there. I'll even ask Lena. She'll tell me."

Ginny wadded her napkin and threw it on the table. "So what if I had a party there?"

Hannah's stomach knotted. She'd been almost sure Ginny wasn't guilty. But she was!

"Who did I hurt?"

"Yourself. And us." Hannah shook her head, still unable to believe Ginny would actually go into a stranger's house and have a party. "How'd you get in?"

Ginny laughed roughly. "It was so simple! Lena and I have been there lots of times."

"What?"

"That shocks you, doesn't it?" Ginny pushed her ugly red hair back. "Maybe I should dye my hair black again. What do you think, Hannah?"

"How'd you get in the house?" Hannah snapped.

"Lena and I sneaked in while you girls were working, then we hid until you left. Sometimes we played hide 'n seek, or we petted the kittens or watched TV."

"But how did you do it yesterday?"

"I unlocked the back door after Chelsea

checked it to make sure it was locked, and then I left it unlocked. When we left last night I locked it."

"But who was there with you?"

Ginny shrugged. "A few kids I met at the park. Some of the neighbor kids."

"And you left all the lights on to make trouble for me, didn't you?" Hannah shook her finger at Ginny.

"Yes! I knew Roxie would suspect you. No matter what she says, she really doesn't like you. She hates all Native Americans."

Hannah's stomach cramped. She was afraid Ginny was speaking the truth. But Roxie had said differently. Hannah bit her lip. She had to believe Roxie no matter how she felt inside. Best friends believed each other. She faced Ginny squarely. "Roxie and I are friends . . . best friends. Nothing you can do will change that."

Ginny's chin quivered, and her eyes filled with tears. She jumped up. "I'm leaving! I don't want to stay here!"

Hannah suddenly realized she didn't mind if Ginny stayed. No matter what, Hannah knew she had best friends who loved her, and she loved them. She loved her family too. Ginny couldn't ruin that.

Slowly Hannah stood up. "You have to stay until your dad says you can go home, Ginny." Hannah fingered the key in the pocket of her shorts. "Want to go with me to the Crandalls'?"

"Why? So you can get your friends to yell at me?"

"They actually like you."

Ginny stood very still. "They do?"

"They thought it was fun to have you at the sleepover."

"They did?"

"They even prayed for you after you left. Chelsea says you're afraid of something." Hannah took a deep breath. "What are you afraid of?"

Ginny groaned and sank to her chair. "Leave me alone!"

Hannah started to leave, then shook her head. "No, Ginny, I won't leave you alone. I want to help you. So does Jesus."

"My dad doesn't believe that."

"Then why did he send you here? He knew my dad would tell you about Jesus."

Ginny trembled. "Uncle has told me Jesus loves me. He showed me in the Bible."

Hannah sat down again and leaned toward Ginny. "I know you are afraid of something. Tell me."

"No!"

"Why are you afraid? Have you told Dad?"

Ginny shook her head. "I . . . just couldn't."

"No matter what it is, he'll help you." Hannah pushed her bowl aside. "Is it . . . your drinking?"

Ginny shook her head hard, then sat quietly.

"Yes," she finally whispered. "I'm so afraid I'll be like Mom and Dad and drink all the time . . . And like Ansell. He told me how bad it is and how awful he feels. What if I get dependent on it like they are?"

"Never take another sip," Hannah said. "If you never touch it, you'll never get dependent on it."

Ginny hung her head. "You make it sound so easy."

"Talk to Dad about it. He'll help you. Honest! He wants to help you."

"I'll . . . I'll think about it."

Hannah jumped up. "I have to get to work now. You can come if you want."

"No. I want to think. I'm going to call my dad and beg him to let me come home."

"Not yet, Ginny. Please! Give my dad a chance to help you. Please?"

Ginny chewed on her bottom lip. "Oh, all right. I'll see what he can do for me. But then I'm leaving."

Hannah laughed in relief. "I'll see you later. If you change your mind, come on down to the Crandalls'. You can pet the kittens."

"They're so cute! I want one."

"Me too, but Mom says no."

"I might stop in." Ginny smiled weakly. "I might."

"Good. See you later." Hannah rushed out and ran all the way to the Crandalls'. Kathy and Roxie were waiting in the yard, laughing and talking. Hannah's heart swelled with happiness as she watched them. They were her friends! It was too good to be true. But it *was* true. What about when school started? She lifted her chin. She'd face that when it came.

"I have the key," Hannah called, holding it up. "Chel couldn't come today."

In a few minutes they stood in the kitchen, and Hannah told them about last night and what Ginny had done. Hannah didn't say anything about Ginny's fear of getting dependent on alcohol. She knew Ginny would be embarrassed if anyone else knew. "She's sorry for having the party and for playing in here other times. She wanted friends and attention . . . Just like Lena did." Hannah told them about Lena and about the missing money.

"We knew you'd solve the mystery," Roxie said with a laugh.

"Detective Hannah," Kathy added, giggling.

With a giggle Hannah told them, "Sorry for talking so long!" It was the most she'd ever talked to anyone. "We have to get done. I'll put out the dogs." She quickly assigned jobs, and they all got to work.

Later as they were leaving Roxie said, "See you this afternoon."

"Do we have a meeting?" Hannah asked in surprise.

"No." Roxie and Kathy exchanged looks.

"Your mom invited us over at 2," Kathy said. "We thought you knew."

Hannah shook her head. What was Mom up to? "Then I'll see you at 2."

At home Hannah found Mom in the kitchen fixing lunch. Ginny was helping her, and Lena and the twins were setting the table. Hannah started to ask her what was going on at 2, but Mom interrupted her.

"I picked your dress up from the cleaners. The stain came out." Mom smiled happily.

Hannah sighed in relief. "I'm glad."

"Ginny has something to tell you." Mom slipped an arm around Ginny and pulled her close. "Ginny?"

Ginny looked down at her feet, took a deep breath, and finally looked at Hannah. "I'll pay the cleaning bill. But I have to make some money. Maybe I could be a *King's Kid* while I'm here and make enough to pay the bill."

Hannah chuckled and nodded. "I'm sure Chelsea will agree."

Lena caught Hannah's hand. "Can't I please be a *King's Kid* too? Mike McCrea is, and he's only eight."

Hannah looked helplessly at Mom, then back down at Lena. "I'll talk to the others."

"Thank you!" Lena hugged Hannah tightly.

Everyone talked at once, and Hannah couldn't find a chance to ask Mom about the plans at two o'clock.

Finally two o'clock came, and the Best Friends all walked in at once.

Mom smiled mysteriously at Hannah and her sisters. "Let's all go down to the basement, shall we?"

Hannah's pulse leaped. Had Mom bought them something really special that she'd hidden in the basement?

"It's nice down here," Ginny said.

Hannah looked all around. The basement looked the same—an area where the little girls played during bad weather and another area where several boxes of stuff were stored. Mostly it was empty. What did Mom have in mind?

"I want to hire all of you *King's Kids* that are here," Mom said. "I want the basement cleared out. We're making it into a huge bedroom/playroom/ study for you girls."

Hannah gasped. Lena and the twins ran around and around, shouting with happiness.

"You'll have your own bathroom," Mom said, opening the bathroom door. "It'll be up to you girls to keep the whole place clean and tidy."

"We will!" they cried together.

Mom laid her arm across Ginny's shoulder.

"This will be your room too while you're here with us."

"Thank you," Ginny whispered.

Hannah looked at the Best Friends, and they burst out laughing. They ran around the room, sharing brilliant ideas on what to do here and there and how to arrange the basement so it would feel like a room for each one.

Hannah ran back to Mom and hugged her tightly. "Thank you, Mom! It's the best surprise in the world."

"I have another one too," Mom said quietly so only Hannah could hear. "Ansell called your dad for help. He'll be here tomorrow."

Hannah's eyes filled with tears as she hugged Mom again. Their prayers were being answered—even the prayer about having a bedroom in the basement.

"Let's get to work," Chelsea said in her "I'm the boss" voice. "Mrs. Shigwam, where do you want these things put?"

"I'll show you. Pick up a box and follow me."

Hannah ran across the room and picked up a box. She was sooo happy! Her best friends were right beside her—right where they'd always be.

You are invited to become a
Best Friends Member!

In becoming a member you'll receive a club membership card with your name on the front and a list of the Best Friends and their favorite Bible verses on the back along with a space for your favorite Scripture. You'll also receive a colorful, 2-inch, specially-made I'M A BEST FRIEND button and a write-up about the author, Hilda Stahl, with her autograph. As a bonus you'll get an occasional newsletter about the upcoming BEST FRIENDS books.

All you need to do is mail your NAME, ADDRESS (printed neatly, please), AGE and $3.00 for postage and handling to:

BEST FRIENDS
P.O. Box 96
Freeport, MI 49325

WELCOME TO THE CLUB!

(Authorized by the author, Hilda Stahl)